JUNIOR DRUG AWARENESS

Ecstasy and Other Club Drugs

JUNIOR DRUG AWARENESS

- Alcohol
- Amphetamines and Other Stimulants
- Cocaine and Crack
- Diet Pills
- Ecstasy and Other Club Drugs
- Heroin
- How to Say No to Drugs
- Inhalants and Solvents
- Marijuana
- Nicotine
- Over-the-Counter Drugs
- Prozac and Other Antidepressants
- Steroids and Other Performance-Enhancing Drugs
- Vicodin, OxyContin, and Other Pain Relievers

JUNIOR DRUG AWARENESS

Ecstasy and Other Club Drugs

Tara Koellhoffer

CHELSEA HOUSE
PUBLISHERS
An imprint of Infobase Publishing

Junior Drug Awareness: Ecstasy and Other Club Drugs
Copyright © 2008 by Infobase Publishing

All rights reserved. No part of this book may be reproduced or utilized in any form or by any means, electronic or mechanical, including photocopying, recording, or by any information storage or retrieval systems, without permission in writing from the publisher. For information contact:

Chelsea House
An imprint of Infobase Publishing
132 West 31st Street
New York NY 10001

Library of Congress Cataloging-in-Publication Data

Koellhoffer, Tara.
 Ecstasy and other club drugs / Tara Koellhoffer.
  p. cm. — (Junior drug awareness)
 Includes bibliographical references and index.
 ISBN-13: 978-0-7910-9697-0 (hardcover)
 ISBN-10: 0-7910-9697-1 (hardcover)
 1. Ecstasy (Drug)—Juvenile literature. 2. Designer drugs—Juvenile literature.
 3. Drug abuse—Juvenile literature. I. Title.

 HV5822.M38K64 2008
 613.8—dc22   2007017789

Chelsea House books are available at special discounts when purchased in bulk quantities for businesses, associations, institutions, or sales promotions. Please call our Special Sales Department in New York at (212) 967-8800 or (800) 322-8755.

You can find Chelsea House on the World Wide Web
at http://www.chelseahouse.com

Text design by Erik Lindstrom
Cover design by Jooyoung An

Printed in the United States of America

Bang PTR 10 9 8 7 6 5 4 3 2 1

This book is printed on acid-free paper.

All links and web addresses were checked and verified to be correct at the time of publication. Because of the dynamic nature of the web, some addresses and links may have changed since publication and may no longer be valid.

CONTENTS

INTRODUCTION
Battling a Pandemic: A History of Drugs
in the United States   6
**by Ronald J. Brogan,
Regional Director of D.A.R.E. America**

1	**Introduction to Club Drugs**	12
2	**Ecstasy (MDMA)**	20
3	**GHB**	35
4	**Rohypnol**	47
5	**Ketamine**	57
6	**LSD**	67
7	**Other Club Drugs**	75
8	**Addiction and Treatment**	86

Glossary	103
Bibliography	107
Further Reading	114
Picture Credits	116
Index	117
About the Authors	120

INTRODUCTION

Battling a Pandemic: A History of Drugs in the United States

When Johnny came marching home again after the Civil War, he probably wasn't marching in a very straight line. This is because Johnny, like 400,000 of his fellow drug-addled soldiers, was addicted to morphine. With the advent of morphine and the invention of the hypodermic needle, drug addiction became a prominent problem during the nineteenth century. It was the first time such widespread drug dependence was documented in history.

Things didn't get much better in the later decades of the nineteenth century. Cocaine and opiates were used as over-the-counter "medicines." Of course, the most famous was Coca-Cola, which actually did contain cocaine in its early days.

After the turn of the twentieth century, drug abuse was spiraling out of control, and the United States government stepped in with the first regulatory controls. In 1906, the Pure Food and Drug Act became a law. It required the labeling of product ingredients. Next came the Harrison Narcotics Tax Act of 1914, which outlawed illegal importation or distribution of cocaine and opiates. During this time, neither the medical community nor the general population was aware of the principles of addiction.

After the passage of the Harrison Act, drug addiction was not a major issue in the United States until the 1960s, when drug abuse became a much bigger social problem. During this time, the federal government's drug enforcement agencies were found to be ineffective. Organizations often worked against one another, causing counterproductive effects. By 1973, things had gotten so bad that President Richard Nixon, by executive order, created the Drug Enforcement Administration (DEA), which became the lead agency in all federal narcotics investigations. It continues in that role to this day. The effectiveness of enforcement and the so-called "Drug War" are open to debate. Cocaine use has been reduced by 75% since its peak in 1985. However, its replacement might be methamphetamine (speed, crank, crystal), which is arguably more dangerous and is now plaguing the country. Also, illicit drugs tend to be cyclical, with various drugs, such as LSD, appearing, disappearing, and then reappearing again. It is probably closest to the truth to say that a war on drugs can never be won, just managed.

Fighting drugs involves a three-pronged battle. Enforcement is one prong. Education and prevention is the second. Treatment is the third.

Although pandemics of drug abuse have been with us for more than 150 years, education and prevention were not seriously considered until the 1970s. In 1982, former First Lady Betty Ford made drug treatment socially acceptable with the opening of the Betty Ford Center. This followed her own battle with addiction. Other treatment centers—including Hazelton, Fair Oaks, and Smithers (now called the Addiction Institute of New York)—added to the growing number of clinics, and soon detox facilities were in almost every city. The cost of a single day in one of these facilities is often more than $1,000, and the effectiveness of treatment centers is often debated. To this day, there is little regulation over who can practice counseling.

It soon became apparent that the most effective way to deal with the drug problem was prevention by education. By some estimates, the overall cost of drug abuse to society exceeds $250 billion per year; preventive education is certainly the most cost-effective way to deal with the problem. Drug education can save people from misery, pain, and ultimately even jail time or death. In the early 1980s, First Lady Nancy Reagan started the "Just Say No" program. Although many scoffed at the program, its promotion of total abstinence from drugs has been effective with many adolescents. In the late 1980s, drug education was not science based, and people essentially were throwing mud at the wall to see what would stick. Motivations of all types spawned hundreds, if not thousands, of drug-education programs. Promoters of some programs used whatever political clout they could muster to get on various government agencies' lists of most effective programs. The bottom line, however, is that prevention is very difficult to quantify. How do you prove that drug use would have occurred if it were not prevented from happening?

In 1983, the Los Angeles Unified School District, in conjunction with the Los Angeles Police Department, started what was considered at that time to be the gold standard of school-based drug education programs. The program was called Drug Abuse Resistance Education, otherwise known as D.A.R.E. The program called for specially trained police officers to deliver drug-education programs in schools. This was an era in which community-oriented policing was all the rage. The logic was that kids would give street credibility to a police officer who spoke to them about drugs. The popularity of the program was unprecedented. It spread all across the country and around the world. Ultimately, 80% of American school districts would utilize the program. Parents, police officers, and kids all loved it. Unexpectedly, a special bond was formed between the kids who took the program and the police officers who ran it. Even in adulthood, many kids remember the name of their D.A.R.E. officer.

By 1991, national drug use had been halved. In any other medical-oriented field, this figure would be astonishing. The number of people in the United States using drugs went from about 25 million in the early 1980s to 11 million in 1991. All three prongs of the battle against drugs vied for government dollars, with each prong claiming credit for the reduction in drug use. There is no doubt that each contributed to the decline in drug use, but most people agreed that preventing drug abuse before it started had proved to be the most effective strategy. The National Institute on Drug Abuse (NIDA), which was established in 1974, defines its mandate in this way: "NIDA's mission is to lead the Nation in bringing the power of science to bear on drug abuse and addiction." NIDA leaders were the experts in prevention and treatment, and they had enormous resources. In

1986, the nonprofit Partnership for a Drug-Free America was founded. The organization defined its mission as, "Putting to use all major media outlets, including TV, radio, print advertisements and the Internet, along with the pro bono work of the country's best advertising agencies." The Partnership for a Drug-Free America is responsible for the popular campaign that compared "your brain on drugs" to fried eggs.

The American drug problem was front-page news for years up until 1990–1991. Then the Gulf War took over the news, and drugs never again regained the headlines. Most likely, this lack of media coverage has led to some peaks and valleys in the number of people using drugs, but there has not been a return to anything near the high percentage of use recorded in 1985. According to the University of Michigan's 2006 Monitoring the Future study, which measured adolescent drug use, there were 840,000 fewer American kids using drugs in 2006 than in 2001. This represents a 23% reduction in drug use. With the exception of prescription drugs, drug use continues to decline.

In 2000, the Robert Wood Johnson Foundation recognized that the D.A.R.E. Program, with its tens of thousands of trained police officers, had the top state-of-the-art delivery system of drug education in the world. The foundation dedicated $15 million to develop a cutting-edge prevention curriculum to be delivered by D.A.R.E. The new D.A.R.E. program incorporates the latest in prevention and education, including high-tech, interactive, and decision-model-based approaches. D.A.R.E. officers are trained as "coaches" who support kids as they practice research-based refusal strategies in high-stakes peer-pressure environments. Through stunning magnetic resonance imaging (MRI) images, students get to see tangible proof of how various substances diminish brain activity.

Will this program be the solution to the drug problem in the United States? By itself, probably not. It is simply an integral part of a larger equation that everyone involved hopes will prevent kids from ever starting to use drugs. The equation also requires guidance in the home, without which no program can be effective.

Ronald J. Brogan
Regional Director
D.A.R.E America

1

Introduction to Club Drugs

Swarms of teens and young adults gather in a warehouse for a rave. Black lights and strobe lights create a flashing, surreal atmosphere. Smoke machines send clouds of fog through the darkness. Teens hold glowsticks as they dance to the pounding beat of the techno music. The crowd seems to move as one giant mass. Many of the partygoers are hugging each other. That's because they are not only affectionate, but also high. The drugs they have taken make them feel **euphoric** and as if they are one with the other people at the rave.

Ten percent of U.S. teens say they have attended a rave—an all-night, underground dance party that is held outdoors or in an empty building. According to teens who have been to raves, drugs are usually available.

Introduction to Club Drugs 13

The main drug taken at raves is Ecstasy. Above, Cathy, a high school student, dances with other ravers at an abandoned warehouse in Portland, Oregon.

The first raves were held in England during the late 1980s. They then spread to the United States and other parts of the world through the efforts of music promoters and entertainers. Most of the early raves were held outdoors or in warehouses. Over time, raves moved into established nightclubs.

European police call raves "drug-taking festivals," and the nickname is fairly accurate. The use of Ecstasy and other so-called club drugs has risen dramatically with the growing popularity of raves. Ironically, raves are often advertised as being "alcohol-free." This label sometimes convinces parents to allow their children to attend the parties, not realizing that many other drugs are available, even if alcohol is not.

In recent years, raves have spread to new locations, and so has the use of club drugs. Many teens today take drugs not just at parties but also at arcades, movie theaters, rock concerts, pool halls, and bowling alleys. To avoid being caught with drugs, teens have devised

CRACKING DOWN ON RAVES

Since raves first became popular in the United States in the 1990s, federal and local governments have been looking for ways to regulate the parties and discourage the use of club drugs. In September 2002 in New Orleans, a rave called "Wild Planet" attracted more than one thousand teens. Also attending the party were several undercover police officers, who monitored the sale and use of drugs and arrested more than a dozen young adults before the rave was over.

Since then, the federal government has passed legislation designed to crack down on raves and the use of club drugs. On April 30, 2003, the RAVE (Reducing Americans' Vulnerability to Ecstasy) Act was passed. The act aimed to "prohibit any individual from knowingly . . . profiting from any place for the purpose of manufacturing, distributing, or using any controlled substance." Congress hailed the law as a first step toward stopping the use of club drugs at raves, but many organizations and people who support or promote raves strongly oppose the law.

inventive ways to hide their stashes, such as keeping pills in Pez or Tic Tac dispensers and storing liquid drugs in water bottles. Some teens even wear strings of drug-laced candies around their necks.

WHICH DRUGS ARE CLUB DRUGS?
Ecstasy

The best known and most common club drug is Ecstasy, or methylenedioxymethamphetamine (MDMA). A **synthetic** substance, Ecstasy has a **psychoactive** effect similar to the effects of the **hallucinogen** mescaline and the **stimulant** methamphetamine.

Ecstasy comes in pill form and is taken orally. Often, the pills are stamped with cute pictures of cartoon characters or other symbols that are familiar to teens and young adults. Because the pills appear to be harmless—especially when compared to other drugs that are smoked or injected with needles—many people who take them don't realize just how dangerous Ecstasy is.

There are many serious health risks associated with Ecstasy use. Users may experience confusion, depression, and sleep problems. Body temperature may rise to dangerous—and even deadly—levels. Heart rate and blood pressure often increase, and users may suffer memory loss, especially if they use Ecstasy over a long period of time.

GHB

Gamma hydroxybutyrate, or GHB, is another popular club drug. It is a central nervous system **depressant**, which means that it slows down the functioning of the brain and nerves. GHB users feel sedated, sleepy, or sometimes euphoric. GHB can be taken in the form of tablets, a powder, or a liquid.

Because GHB can sedate people so heavily that they are unaware of what is going on around them, GHB is often referred to as a "date rape drug." A sexual predator slips GHB into a victim's drink, waits for its effects to kick in (which usually happens about 10 to 20 minutes after the victim ingests the drug), and then takes advantage of the victim's inability to stop sexual advances. GHB is also an effective date rape drug because all traces of it leave the body in just a few hours. By the time a victim realizes what has happened, there is no evidence that he or she has been given the drug.

Even if a person takes GHB willingly, there are serious risks. In large doses, it can sedate someone so strongly that he or she may fall into a coma, or even die.

Rohypnol

Rohypnol is a **benzodiazepine**, part of a class of drugs used to treat sleep disorders and anxiety. However, Rohypnol is not on the list of legal benzodiazepines in the United States. In some other countries, it is used to treat **insomnia** and as an **anesthetic** before surgery.

Rohypnol is colorless and has no odor, which makes it, like GHB, another popular date rape drug. It can be slipped into a drink. It will cause the victim to become drowsy, dizzy, and confused. Even when taken in very small doses, it can leave a person delirious or heavily sedated for up to 12 hours. Other risks associated with Rohypnol include low blood pressure, severe dizziness, stomach upset, and occasional visual hallucinations.

Ketamine

Ketamine is used legally as an anesthetic, usually by veterinarians. Yet, it has become a popular illegal drug at raves. It can be injected, smoked, or snorted. Ketamine is yet another club drug that is a notorious date rape drug. Like GHB and Rohypnol, it is often slipped into a person's drink by a sexual predator.

Ketamine can cause attention deficits and memory problems. At higher doses, users may experience symptoms similar to those seen with **phencyclidine (PCP)** use, such as hallucinations, dream-like states, or delirium. Even higher doses of Ketamine may cause high blood pressure, depression, and severe breathing problems, which may lead to death.

LSD

Unlike other club drugs, which became popular only in recent decades, **lysergic acid diethylamide (LSD)** has been in fairly widespread use since the early 1960s. It was made illegal in the United States in 1967. It remains a popular recreational drug, particularly among the "hippies" of the 1960s and 1970s counterculture.

LSD is a hallucinogen: Users see and hear things that are not really there. LSD is sold in many forms, from blotter paper to gelatin squares to tablets. Sometimes it is even sold on sugar cubes.

People experience different reactions to LSD. Some users sweat, have trouble sleeping, and feel weak or numb. Other users may have a rise in heart rate, dry mouth, and tremors. People who use LSD regularly may experience **psychosis** and **flashbacks**. Flashbacks are hallucinations that occur months, or even years, after a person stops taking the drug.

Other Club Drugs

Several club drugs are becoming more popular among young people. These include

- Methamphetamine, an addictive drug that stimulates the central nervous system
- Dextromethorphan (DXM), a cough suppressant that can cause hallucinations

18 ECSTASY AND OTHER CLUB DRUGS

One popular way to use LSD is with blotter paper. The paper is usually covered with eye-catching graphics and is perforated into individual tabs or hits. The sheets are then dipped in LSD.

- 2CB, a synthetic **psychedelic** drug
- 4-MTA, a strong stimulant
- Chloral hydrate, a sleep-inducing depressant

ABUSE AND ADDICTION

Drug abuse can be defined as the use of any illegal substance, or the excessive use of a substance that is available by prescription from a medical professional or over the counter. Most club drugs are illegal or are available only with a prescription. People who take these substances at raves or other hangouts are abusing drugs.

People who abuse drugs over a period of time can become dependent on, or addicted to, these drugs. With long-term drug use, the body develops a **tolerance** for the drug. This means that users have to take more of the drug to achieve the same high that they used to experience when they first started taking it. Eventually, they need to take the drug just to feel normal. If an addicted person stops taking the drug or tries to go for a period of time without it, he or she will suffer **withdrawal** symptoms. These may include strong cravings for the drug, headaches, irritability, nervousness, and problems sleeping.

Physical effects are only one part of drug **addiction**. Many drug users also experience **psychological dependence** on the drug. Even if the body doesn't physically crave the drug, a person may become so used to the habit of taking it that he or she will have trouble going without the substance. Although studies show that some club drugs may be more addictive than others, all of them can be habit-forming, and all of them may lead to psychological dependence. Along with the many physical risks associated with club drugs, becoming psychologically hooked is a risk not worth taking.

2

Ecstasy (MDMA)

Viola had been looking forward to attending the party for a long time. As soon as she got there, she bought two Ecstasy pills from a friend and took them. Instead of experiencing the euphoric high she had been expecting, Viola fell into a stupor. She ended up sitting by herself for an hour, feeling so confused that she couldn't tell if she was happy or sad. She knew she must have looked bad, because people kept coming up to her and giving her water. After about four hours of sitting alone, feeling her eyes roll back into her head, she started to feel better and got up and danced. Finally, it seemed like the Ecstasy was kicking in. After she got home, however, she went right to bed. She hardly moved or spoke at all for three days after the party. It was a terrifying experience.

Viola posted the true story of her experiment with Ecstasy online because she wanted to let other people know how scary taking the drug can be. Not every experience with Ecstasy is exactly like Viola's, though. In fact, it's almost impossible to predict how any particular person will react to this popular club drug.

WHAT IS ECSTASY?

The chemical name for Ecstasy is methylenedioxymethamphetamine, or MDMA for short. Ecstasy is a synthetic substance: It is man-made and does not occur naturally. Depending on the way it is made, Ecstasy can be classified as either a stimulant or a hallucinogen. In low doses, Ecstasy stimulates the central nervous system, but in larger doses, it can cause hallucinations.

Methylenedioxyamphetamine, or MDA, is a drug closely related to Ecstasy. Merck, a drug company, first created MDA in Germany in 1910. Some people believe it was sold as an appetite suppressant, but many historians consider this a myth. MDMA was produced in 1912. In the years after it was first synthesized, MDMA was largely ignored. That was because of the outbreak of World War I, which forced the pharmaceutical industry to focus on drugs and other chemicals that could aid the war effort.

In 1941, scientists tested MDA as a treatment for **Parkinson's disease**, but it caused muscle stiffness in at least one of the patients involved in the experiment, so the study was discontinued. Still, scientists continued to experiment with MDA and the drugs related to it, including MDMA. In the 1950s, the U.S. military briefly considered MDMA as a possibility in its search for a "truth serum" that could make interrogations easier.

American chemist Alexander Shulgin is responsible for developing and promoting MDMA, most commonly known as Ecstasy. He tested its use in treating depression and post-traumatic stress disorder.

In 1967, American chemist Alexander Shulgin was introduced to MDMA by one of his graduate students. Shulgin began to experiment with the drug and came up with a new way to make it. During the 1970s and early 1980s, Shulgin promoted the drug as an aid in talk therapy and marriage counseling. He found that it reduced hostility between people.

During the years that Shulgin was using MDMA as part of psychiatric therapy, many people began to use the drug recreationally. Concerned about the potential dangers of the drug when used without medical supervision, the United States banned MDMA in 1985. Nevertheless, its use as an illicit drug continued, especially as raves became popular through the late 1980s and 1990s.

At the same time, scientists continued to experiment with MDMA, searching for ways to use the drug to treat various illnesses. In recent years, several studies have been done to see if MDMA might be useful in the treatment of **posttraumatic stress disorder (PTSD)**. PTSD occurs in people who have been exposed to a traumatic event, such as war, a natural disaster, or rape. Sufferers often experience anxiety, depression, and flashbacks of the traumatic incident. One of the organizations conducting studies of MDMA and PTSD is the Multidisciplinary Association for Psychedelic Studies (MAPS). MAPS scientists believe that MDMA might help PTSD victims feel more comfortable talking about their feelings with a therapist because MDMA works on the emotion centers of the brain. Although the MAPS studies and others have shown some promise, few scientists believe that the U.S. government will approve MDMA as a legitimate drug treatment. That's because the government has spent years making people aware of MDMA as a potentially dangerous recreational drug.

HOW IS ECSTASY USED?

Ecstasy is a white powder. It is most often produced as a capsule or tablet form and taken by mouth. A user may also snort or smoke the powder, or even inject it with a needle. These methods are less common.

The average Ecstasy dose is between 100 and 150 milligrams. One dose normally costs $10 to $30 when purchased illegally at clubs or raves.

Ecstasy pills come in many different forms. The pills may be colored and almost always have a symbol stamped on them, and this symbol is usually well known to young people. One example is the cartoon character

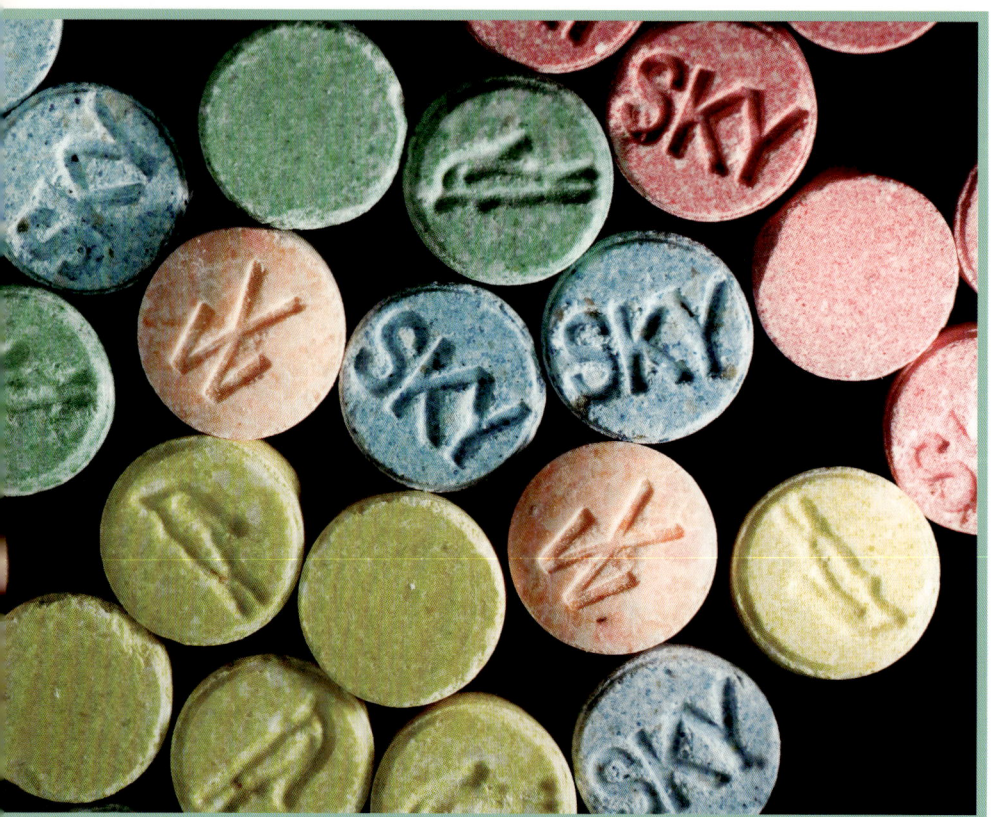

Ecstasy can be swallowed, snorted, smoked, or injected. In tablet form, the drug is usually imprinted with unique signs or symbols so that different makers can distinguish their drugs from other makers' drugs.

Tweety Bird. New designs are constantly being produced. According to some sources, at least six new types of Ecstasy pills enter the illegal market every month.

The user usually starts to feel the effects of Ecstasy about 45 minutes after taking the drug. If the drug is snorted, smoked, or injected, the effects normally kick in sooner. An Ecstasy high can last anywhere from three to eight hours, and sometimes longer.

Although the high that Ecstasy produces can vary from person to person, there are a few common effects. People report that they feel happier than usual and have more energy for dancing. Many users say that they feel as if everything is all right and that they are "one with the world" while high on Ecstasy. Another common effect is **empathogenesis**: a sense of being emotionally close to other people, even strangers. Ecstasy can make users feel more comfortable in social situations. Many people take it if they tend to be shy or awkward at parties or other social events.

The euphoric feelings don't last for long. After the high, Ecstasy produces a "burnout" effect. A user "crashes," or tends to feel tired, sore, and both mentally and physically sluggish for a day or two after taking the drug.

HOW ECSTASY AFFECTS THE BODY
Short-term Effects

Ecstasy works by increasing the levels of certain **neurotransmitters** in the brain. The three main neurotransmitters that are affected are **serotonin**, **norepinephrine**, and **dopamine**. Ecstasy causes more of these neurotransmitters to be released in the brain. This increases the brain's activity and stimulates the nervous system. Serotonin is involved in regulating mood, as well as pain, sleep, and appetite. Ecstasy causes the brain to release serotonin, improving the user's mood in the short term. However, it also blocks the brain cells' ability to take serotonin back inside themselves for later use, which actually depletes the level of serotonin that is available to boost the person's mood naturally when he or she isn't taking Ecstasy. Over time, this lack of serotonin can lead to long-term mood problems.

Eventually, the person needs to take Ecstasy in order to feel good.

Ecstasy causes a wide variety of physical effects soon after it is ingested. Users can become overexcited, nervous, and dizzy. A person's heart rate can increase to dangerous levels. Physical symptoms that often occur with Ecstasy use include muscle tension, nausea, blurred vision, teeth grinding, and jaw clenching. Some teens chew on pacifiers while high on Ecstasy to avoid grinding

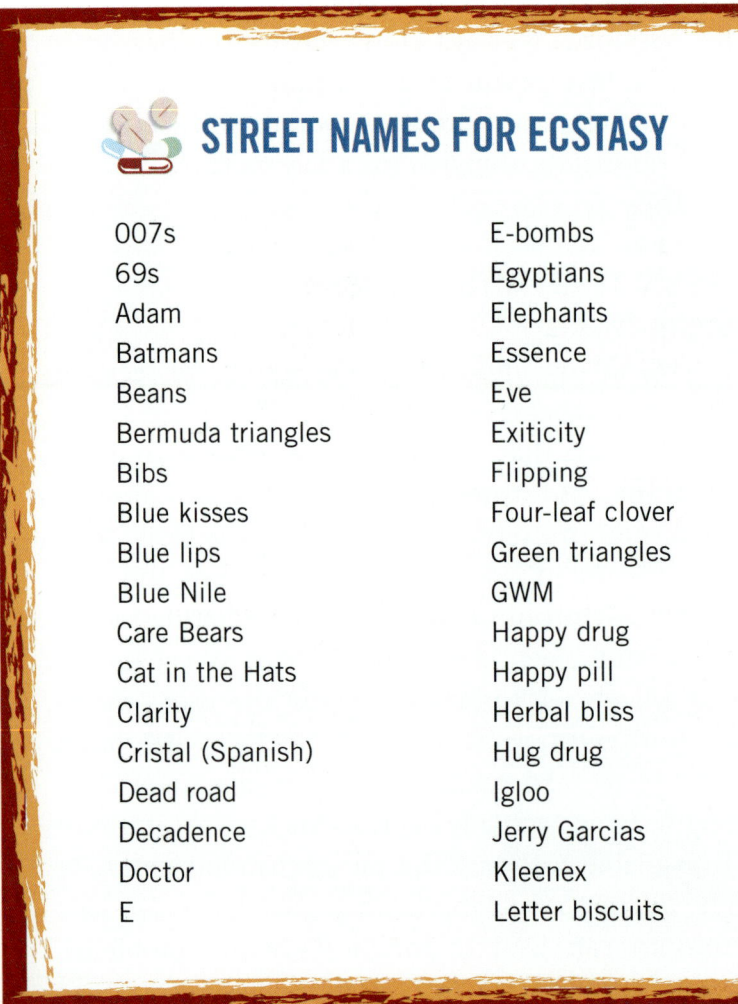

STREET NAMES FOR ECSTASY

007s	E-bombs
69s	Egyptians
Adam	Elephants
Batmans	Essence
Beans	Eve
Bermuda triangles	Exiticity
Bibs	Flipping
Blue kisses	Four-leaf clover
Blue lips	Green triangles
Blue Nile	GWM
Care Bears	Happy drug
Cat in the Hats	Happy pill
Clarity	Herbal bliss
Cristal (Spanish)	Hug drug
Dead road	Igloo
Decadence	Jerry Garcias
Doctor	Kleenex
E	Letter biscuits

their teeth. Still, one study reported that 60% of Ecstasy users had worn through the enamel on their teeth.

Many users sweat, and some talk incessantly. Ecstasy has strong effects on the cardiovascular system and on the body's ability to maintain a normal temperature. Taking Ecstasy at raves is often combined with long periods of vigorous dancing. This can cause the body to become much warmer than normal, which can lead to a condition called **hyperthermia**. The heart and kidneys

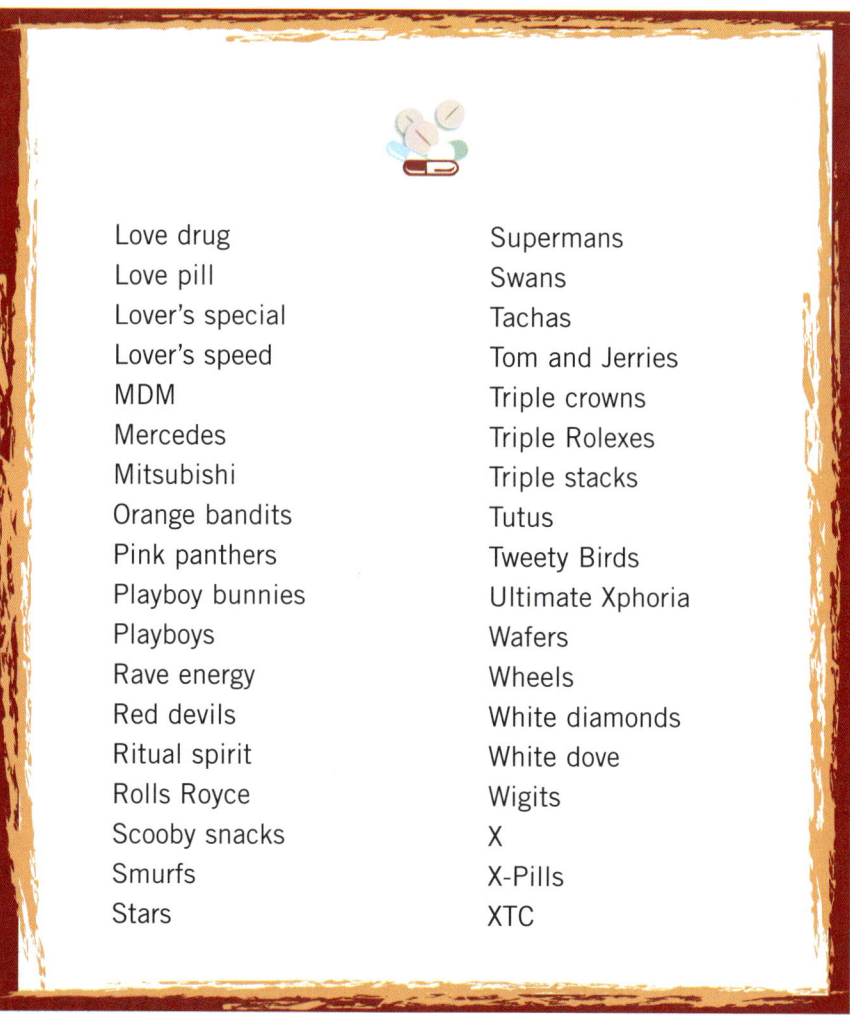

Love drug
Love pill
Lover's special
Lover's speed
MDM
Mercedes
Mitsubishi
Orange bandits
Pink panthers
Playboy bunnies
Playboys
Rave energy
Red devils
Ritual spirit
Rolls Royce
Scooby snacks
Smurfs
Stars

Supermans
Swans
Tachas
Tom and Jerries
Triple crowns
Triple Rolexes
Triple stacks
Tutus
Tweety Birds
Ultimate Xphoria
Wafers
Wheels
White diamonds
White dove
Wigits
X
X-Pills
XTC

28   ECSTASY AND OTHER CLUB DRUGS

Drug users usually take Ecstasy for its euphoric effects. The drug is also known to increase tactile sensations, making physical touch more pleasurable. Once the drug has taken its course, the user crashes and feels tired and sluggish. Here, an Ecstasy user named Lara lies on her couch with a friend during a night of partying in New York City.

break down, particularly when the user does not drink enough water to replenish the fluids lost through sweat.

Ecstasy can cause seizures or strokes. A few reports have indicated that Ecstasy may cause uncontrolled bleeding, perhaps because the drug prevents blood from clotting. Although it is rare, Ecstasy has also caused death in some users, often because of an unexpected heart attack.

Long-term Effects

Chronic use of Ecstasy can cause many unpleasant and dangerous symptoms. Ecstasy can damage the parts of the brain that are involved in processing memories. People who use Ecstasy over time often suffer from dehydration, hypertension (high blood pressure), heart failure, kidney failure, and hyperthermia. Many habitual users also suffer from insomnia.

Studies on the effects of Ecstasy show some interesting findings. One research study took images of people's brains before they took Ecstasy and again two weeks after taking the drug. The blood flow in their brains was much less apparent after taking the drug. Other studies have shown that Ecstasy users tend to achieve

IS ECSTASY DANGEROUS TO FIRST-TIME USERS?

A controversial study presented at the November 2006 meeting of the Radiological Society of North America (RSNA) stated that Ecstasy could be harmful to the brains of people who have used it only one time. Dr. Maartje de Win of the University of Amsterdam led the study. De Win and her colleagues examined 188 volunteers who had never used Ecstasy but who were at high risk for trying the drug. Eighteen months later, they examined the same people. By then, 59 of the volunteers had tried Ecstasy. They each had taken an average of six tablets. These people had small changes in the way their brain cells were structured. They also had less blood flow in the brain than they did before they had taken Ecstasy. The researchers admitted that they could not know if these changes in the brain were permanent. But their findings suggest that even a single experiment with Ecstasy can cause damage to the brain.

lower scores on tests that involve attention, learning, and memory. Besides affecting the thinking processes of the brain, Ecstasy acts on the mood and emotional centers of the brain, causing long-term users to experience depression, anxiety, **paranoia**, and other psychological problems.

Some animal studies have found that a brain on Ecstasy demonstrates symptoms similar to those of patients with **Alzheimer's disease**, including damage to nerve terminals. Because scientists are just now beginning to see the long-term effects of Ecstasy, it is possible that people may suffer brain damage, and even experience suicidal depression, 10 to 15 years after using the drug.

ABUSE AND DEPENDENCE

Most scientists agree that Ecstasy is not physically addictive. But users still can become dependent on the drug. Many drug treatment and rehabilitation centers have reported an increase in the number of patients seeking help in dealing with a psychological need for Ecstasy.

Seventeen-year-old Daniel first took Ecstasy on prom night, hoping to make the night one to remember. Soon after taking a couple of pills, he felt his heart racing and worried that he might be having a heart attack. The panic went away, though, and Daniel started to enjoy the high, saying he felt like a movie star. After the prom, Daniel began to crash. Feeling confused and sad, he took more Ecstasy. That was the beginning of Daniel's dependence.

Instead of being a one-night event, Daniel began to take Ecstasy every weekend. Before long, he was taking as many as five Ecstasy pills each day. He had developed a very expensive habit, and he became distressed whenever he thought he might not be able to get the drug. To pay for his daily dose of Ecstasy, he started to sell other drugs and began to steal from his parents. A few months later, Daniel had an argument with his girlfriend, and she called him a drug addict. Daniel realized that he needed help to stop taking Ecstasy. He checked into a drug treatment center and learned how to live without drugs.

Daniel was a typical Ecstasy user. Like Daniel, most people who take Ecstasy are young (in their teens to mid-twenties). Most are educated: They are in, or have graduated from, high school, and many have a college education as well. Unlike crack or heroin users, most Ecstasy users are young adults who have never been in trouble with the law. Although most Ecstasy users only take the drug occasionally, at parties or other special events, it is easy to see from Daniel's true story—posted on the Web site of the National Institute on Drug Abuse—how easily a person can cross the line from recreational use of the drug into dependence.

DANGERS OF ECSTASY USE

In addition to the physical and psychological effects that Ecstasy can cause, there are other dangers. First, there is the danger of criminal prosecution. The U.S. government puts all drugs into schedules, or categories, based on how addictive they are and what legitimate medical uses they have. Ecstasy is a Schedule I drug, which means that it is considered to have *no* acceptable uses by the federal government. Other Schedule I drugs include heroin and crack cocaine. Because Ecstasy is illegal, being caught using it or possessing it is a serious crime that can result in jail time.

Besides the possible criminal implications of using Ecstasy, it is important to remember that no government or medical agency oversees its production. That

THE CONTROLLED SUBSTANCES ACT

The Controlled Substances Act of 1970 places all drugs into one of five categories, or schedules, depending on their use and potential for abuse.

SCHEDULE I:
- The drug has a high potential for abuse.
- The drug has no currently accepted medical use in the United States.
- The drug is not safe to use, even under medical supervision.
- Examples of Schedule I drugs include Ecstasy, GHB, heroin, and LSD.

SCHEDULE II:
- The drug has a high potential for abuse.
- The drug either has no currently accepted medical use in the United States or has a currently accepted medical use with severe restrictions about who may use the drug and in what circumstances.
- Abuse of the drug may lead to severe psychological or physical dependence.
- Examples of Schedule II drugs include morphine, Ritalin, phencyclidine (PCP), and methadone.

SCHEDULE III:
- The drug or other substance has a potential for abuse less than the drugs or other substances in Schedules I and II.
- The drug or other substance has a currently accepted medical use in the United States.

- Abuse of the drug or other substance may lead to moderate or low physical dependence or high psychological dependence.
- Examples of Schedule III drugs include anabolic steroids, codeine, and some barbiturates.

SCHEDULE IV:
- The drug or other substance has a low potential for abuse relative to the drugs or other substances in Schedule III.
- The drug or other substance has a currently accepted medical use in the United States.
- Abuse of the drug or other substance may lead to limited physical dependence or psychological dependence relative to the drugs or other substances in Schedule III.
- Examples of Schedule IV drugs include Phenobarbital, Xanax, and Valium.

SCHEDULE V:
- The drug or other substance has a low potential for abuse relative to the drugs or other substances in Schedule IV.
- The drug or other substance has a currently accepted medical use in the United States.
- Abuse of the drug or other substance may lead to limited physical dependence or psychological dependence relative to the drugs or other substances in Schedule IV.
- Examples of Schedule V drugs include cough suppressants.

means that the drug dealers who make and sell Ecstasy can put anything into the pills. Drug dealers often add cheaper chemicals to their drugs to keep costs low and maximize profits. In many cases, these "impure" Ecstasy pills can be even more hazardous to ingest than Ecstasy itself. It is impossible to predict the symptoms that these impure pills may produce, and it is easy for users to unknowingly poison themselves. Many overdoses and fatalities associated with Ecstasy are the result of impure pills.

3

GHB

Leigh was at a party at a friend's house. While she was hanging around with two of her friends, an acquaintance came up to them with a bottle of liquid GHB. He told them there was enough in the bottle for all three of them. After he walked away, they decided there was only enough for one dose, so Leigh drank it all herself. After a few minutes, she started to feel drunk. Soon, she could not walk without help. Her friends had to drag her from room to room. Even so, she was enjoying the feeling of intoxication. She later remembered sitting on a bed, talking about music and tossing a ball around with her friends. Unfortunately, that's the last thing she remembered. Leigh woke up a day later in the hospital with a breathing tube down her throat. Her friends told her she had suddenly stopped talking and passed out. Then, she stopped breathing. Luckily, one of her friends knows **CPR** and was able to save her life before the ambulance arrived. Leigh posted the story of her real-life experience online to warn other young people about the dangers of GHB.

Although many GHB users report only mild effects when they take small doses of the drug, even the most experienced users say that it is very easy to accidentally overdose, as Leigh did.

WHAT IS GHB?

GHB is short for gamma hydroxybutyrate. The form used as a club drug is a powerful, synthetically produced depressant that affects the central nervous system. However, GHB also exists naturally in the body. It is produced in the brain by a neurotransmitter called **gamma-aminobutyric acid (GABA)**. GHB is found in several parts of the human brain, particularly the **thalamus**, the **hypothalamus**, and the **substantia nigra**.

To produce synthetic GHB, a chemical called GBL (an industrial solvent often used to clean floors) is mixed with lye or drain cleaner. GHB was first made in the 1920s. By the 1960s, scientists were studying it as a possible anesthetic. But research showed that it was not very good at preventing pain, so it never became a popular form of anesthesia.

However, while they were researching GHB, scientists noticed that it caused the body to release **human growth hormone**. This hormone helps the muscles develop. This discovery made GHB appealing to weight lifters and body builders. Many athletes began to use GHB, which was then available as a dietary supplement, to increase their muscle mass.

GHB, otherwise known as "liquid Ecstasy" is shown in different containers that were confiscated by police. GHB effects include euphoria, drowsiness, and unconsciousness. It is commonly referred to as a "date rape" drug. When mixed with alcohol, it is entirely odorless and tasteless, and it causes the victim to be unable to resist or remember the attack.

By the late 1980s, there were many reports about illnesses linked with GHB. Symptoms ranged from nausea to seizures and slipping into a coma. The Food and Drug Administration (FDA) began to study the drug in 1990. In March 2000, GHB became illegal in the United States, although it is still used in a few European countries to improve the functions of other anesthetics.

GHB is a Schedule I drug, but research is being done to determine whether it has any legitimate medical uses. One of the most promising uses for GHB is for the treatment of **narcolepsy**, a sleep disorder. In 2002, the FDA approved Xyrem, a drug that contains GHB as an active ingredient, for use in treating **cataplexy** attacks in narcolepsy patients.

HOW IS GHB USED?

GHB is most often taken by mouth. It is usually sold as a liquid. Liquid GHB is colorless, has no odor, and has a slightly soapy or salty taste. When it is mixed with a beverage, it is almost entirely tasteless. GHB also is sold as a light-colored powder that is made into capsules.

At clubs and raves, GHB is usually sold as a liquid in water bottles, vials, or even water guns. Occasionally, dealers will sell lollipops or other candies that have been dipped in GHB. Users normally take GHB by the capful or teaspoonful. An average dose is between 1 gram and 5 grams, and generally costs $5 to $10.

A user begins to feel the effects of GHB 15 to 30 minutes after ingesting the drug, and the high usually lasts 3 to 6 hours. GHB makes the user feel euphoric and relaxed, similar to the way a person feels after drinking alcohol. In larger doses, however, the drug can cause dangerous physical problems. Its effects depend on the dose. If a person takes less than 1 gram, GHB tends to act as a relaxant. The muscles loosen and the person becomes less inhibited, as often occurs with alcohol. Taking 1 to 2 grams produces a stronger sense of relaxation, and the heart and breathing rates slow down. If the user takes 2 to 4 grams, the drug begins to cause problems with speech and movement. At higher doses, the user may fall into a deep sleep or even a coma. Taking GHB with alcohol (which is often done at raves and other parties) makes the drug an even stronger depressant that can cause serious breathing problems, unconsciousness, or even death.

EFFECTS OF GHB
Short-term Effects

GHB exists naturally in the brain. So when synthetic GHB is taken, it affects several neurotransmitter systems. Levels of serotonin and **acetylcholine** increase, while dopamine activity decreases.

Other short-term effects of GHB include nausea and vomiting, hallucinations, **vertigo**, delusions, depression, lowered blood pressure, **amnesia**, and loss of consciousness. The user may feel weak and have trouble breathing, and may suffer from **bradycardia**, confusion, and agitation. Taking GHB can also cause the user to lose his or her **peripheral vision** and become uncoordinated. These effects normally go away about seven hours after taking the drug, but the user may continue to feel dizzy for as long as two weeks.

STREET NAMES FOR GHB

Cherry Meth
Easy lay
Fantasy
G-riffic
Gamma Oh
GBH
Georgia home boy
Goop
Great hormones at bedtime
Grievous bodily harm
Jib

Liquid E
Liquid Ecstasy
Liquid G
Liquid X
Organic Quaalude
Salty water
Scoop
Sleep
Sleep-500
Somatomax

Combining GHB with alcohol or other drugs dramatically increases the dangerous short-term effects on the body. Unfortunately, many users habitually take GHB with other substances. Other drug abusers and many Internet sites claim to teach users how to safely mix drugs. This misinformation may encourage people to experiment with GHB and other drugs, which can lead to frequent recreational use and even more physical problems over the long term.

Long-term Effects

GHB can become addictive if it is used over a long period of time. People who have used GHB every day for at least two months have shown signs of addiction and have experienced withdrawal symptoms when they stopped using the drug. Those who use GHB every two to four hours for several days experience withdrawal symptoms, too. These include insomnia, anxiety, **tachycardia**, tremors, and agitation. Some people suffer more severe effects, including delirium, psychosis, severe sweating, and hallucinations.

GHB works quickly and leaves the body rapidly. Because of this, users may experience withdrawal symptoms one to six hours after their last dose. These unpleasant symptoms may last anywhere from 5 to 15 days. Some people who are coming off a long period of GHB use have temporary memory loss. Because this can be so frustrating, many people start taking GHB again to make it go away. Withdrawal from GHB can be severe. People who've taken GHB for a long time have died from heart problems after stopping the drug. People who go through a medically supervised detoxification program need to be hospitalized, usually for 7 to 14 days.

WHO USES GHB?

Young adults are the most common GHB users. Many try the drug because they have read on the Internet that GHB is harmless and doesn't cause addiction or overdose. The typical GHB user is a white, middle-class male between the ages of 13 and 30. Taken most often at clubs and parties, GHB is commonly used with other drugs, especially alcohol and Ecstasy. According to the University of Michigan's Monitoring the Future Survey, 1.6% of twelfth graders admitted that they had used GHB, and several cities across the United States have reported

MICHIGAN PROCLAIMS MARCH AS GHB AWARENESS MONTH

In 2001, as reports of GHB use and abuse were becoming more prevalent, the Michigan Department of Community Health designated March as GHB Awareness Month. Spokesperson Susan Shafer said that the Michigan Women's Commission, the Michigan Police Commission, and the governor's office had been working with local community health groups for two years to find a way to make people more aware of the dangers of GHB as a date rape drug and club drug. After three University of Michigan students overdosed on GHB in the fall of 2000, state officials realized that something had to be done soon. Part of GHB Awareness Month is to instruct people that GHB can be dangerous when it is taken as a recreational drug, as well as when it is slipped into an unwitting person's drink.

increases in GHB use over the last several years. In some regions, a rise in GHB use corresponded to a rise in the number of raves, indicating that GHB is indeed becoming an increasingly popular club drug.

DANGERS OF GHB USE

Taking GHB itself can be harmful, but the drug becomes even more dangerous when it is used alongside other recreational drugs. Mixing drugs can increase the risk of overdose. Each year, thousands of GHB users go to the emergency room because of bad reactions to the drug. Since 1990, more than 15,000 cases of GHB overdoses and more than 70 deaths due to GHB use have been documented by the U.S. Drug Enforcement Administration (DEA).

GHB is a problem not only because of the physical effects it produces. As a Schedule I drug, GHB is illegal to use or possess, and being caught with it can lead to jail time and/or heavy fines. The one legitimate product that contains GHB, the narcolepsy drug Xylem, is heavily monitored. Using or possessing Xylem without a doctor's prescription is a criminal act.

GHB AS A DATE RAPE DRUG

One of the most common dangers associated with GHB is date rape. Because GHB is usually odorless and tasteless when mixed with a drink, it is easy for a sexual predator to slip it into a victim's drink without the drug being noticed. That is what happened to Samantha Reid, whose true story can be found on the Web site of the PBS program *NewsHour*.

Samantha was a 15-year-old high school freshman who lived near Detroit. One night in January 1999, while she was with friends at a party, she asked for a Mountain Dew. A 19-year-old boy brought her the drink,

GHB often causes a person to fall into a coma-like sleep, which is what happened to this girl who passed out at a Dutch music festival. Users draw a large "G" on their palms to indicate that they have taken the drug. This helps others know why these individuals may slip into deep sleeps.

(From left to right) **Nicholas Holtschlag, Erick Limmer, Daniel Brayman, and Joshua Cole sit in a courtroom on February 14, 2000, as they stand trial for the poisoning death of Samantha Reid. The 15-year-old girl died after the four men allegedly spiked her drink with GHB. Their case is believed to be the first prosecution of a GHB-related death in the United States.**

which she said tasted "gross" while she was drinking it. After a short while, she vomited and then passed out. She fell into a coma and never regained consciousness. Samantha died at the hospital the next day. It turned out that the boy who gave her the Mountain Dew had "scooped" her drink. *Scooping* is a street term for slipping GHB into someone's beverage. In February 2000, four young men were convicted of Samantha's murder. It was the first trial for a death related to GHB use. According to a statement made by one of the convicted young men, they thought that slipping a little bit of GHB into Samantha's drink would "liven" her up.

Although Samantha Reid was able to taste the GHB that had been put in her Mountain Dew, in most cases, the taste of the beverage masks the flavor of the drug. The victim never realizes she has been drugged until it is too late. GHB is an especially effective date rape drug because only a small amount is needed to make the victim lose consciousness and become unable to defend

THE HILLORY J. FARIAS AND SAMANTHA REID DATE-RAPE DRUG PROHIBITION ACT OF 2000

After Samantha Reid died of a GHB overdose, Congress passed the Hillory J. Farias and Samantha Reid Date-Rape Drug Prohibition Act of 2000. Hillory Farias was another teenage girl who died after GHB was slipped into her drink. President Clinton signed the legislation on February 18, 2000.

The law made GHB a Schedule I controlled substance, which means that it has a high potential for abuse. The act makes it a crime to possess nonmedical GHB and imposes stiff penalties for selling the drug. If someone is caught with GHB in his or her possession, the person may be sentenced to a year in prison and a fine of $1,000. If a person is convicted of selling or providing GHB to someone else, he or she may be sentenced to up to 20 years in prison. In addition, if someone dies because of GHB, the person who gave it to him or her can receive the death penalty.

himself or herself against a sexual assault. The drug also causes amnesia, so the victim is often left with no memory of what happened, making it difficult for her to seek help right after the sexual assault. In addition, GHB moves quickly through the body. It is often impossible to detect just a few hours after it has been ingested. This makes it difficult to prove that the victim has been drugged. According to the National Drug Intelligence Center (NDIC), GHB is now the most common date rape drug.

Rohypnol

Stella (not her real name) thought it would be fun to go with some of her college friends across the Mexican border to Tijuana. The night started out fine. The girls were having a great time shopping and exploring the city. But then they stopped at a restaurant to have a few drinks. The waiter offered them some pills that he said were great with alcohol. Thinking the pills were painkillers that would just make them a little more intoxicated, Stella and her friends tried the pills. By the time they were ready to leave Tijuana, they could hardly walk. Soon after they reached the United States, the police found them almost passed out in a parking lot, and one of Stella's friends was arrested because she still had some of the pills they had taken. It was only because of the arrest that the girls found out what drug they had taken: Rohypnol, a well-known date rape drug. The girls realized that the waiter who gave them the pills was a sexual predator. They felt lucky to have made it back to the United States without being sexually assaulted. To make sure that other people would know about the risks of Rohypnol, Stella posted her true story online.

WHAT IS ROHYPNOL?

Rohypnol's chemical name is flunitrazepam. It is a type of benzodiazepine, a drug that acts as a central nervous system depressant and is used to manage anxiety. Rohypnol is similar to the well-known sedative Valium, but it is 5 to 10 times more powerful.

Hoffman-La Roche Inc., a drug company, first produced Rohypnol in the 1970s to help people sleep and to sedate patients. In 1975, Rohypnol entered the commercial market in Europe. By the 1980s, its use was spreading to other countries, including the United States. It was also in the 1980s that the first reports of Rohypnol abuse began to surface. From Asia to Los Angeles, heroin addicts were using Rohypnol to make the effects of heroin last longer. Soon, crack and cocaine addicts also began to use Rohypnol because it helped them come down from drug binges. In the United States, many people take Rohypnol to increase the effects of alcohol, marijuana, and other drugs.

As reports of Rohypnol abuse continued, the United States moved to make the drug illegal. In 1995, Rohypnol was placed on Schedule III of the 1971 Convention of Psychotropic Substances and was designated a Schedule IV drug. This designation means that it has some medical use. However, it is illegal to import Rohypnol into the

STREET NAMES FOR ROHYPNOL

Circles
Forget-me pill
Forget pill
La rocha
Lunch money drug
Mexican valium
Pingus
R-2
Reynolds
Roach-2
Roaches
Roachies

Roapies
Robutal
Rochas dos
Rope
Rophies
Rophy
Ropies
Roples
Row-shay
Ruffies
Wolfies

United States, and the drug is also part of a list of date rape drugs under the October 1996 Drug-Induced Rape Prevention and Punishment Act. Currently, Rohypnol is being considered for placement on the U.S. Schedule I drug list. That indicates that the drug has a high potential for abuse and no medical uses. Several states, including Florida, Idaho, New Mexico, North Dakota, and Minnesota, have already placed Rohypnol on their state Schedule I drug lists.

Although Rohypnol has no accepted medical uses in the United States, it is still used as a legitimate sleeping pill in Mexico, South America, Asia, and Europe. About 60 countries around the world allow legal use of Rohypnol. In England, the drug is available by prescription. It also

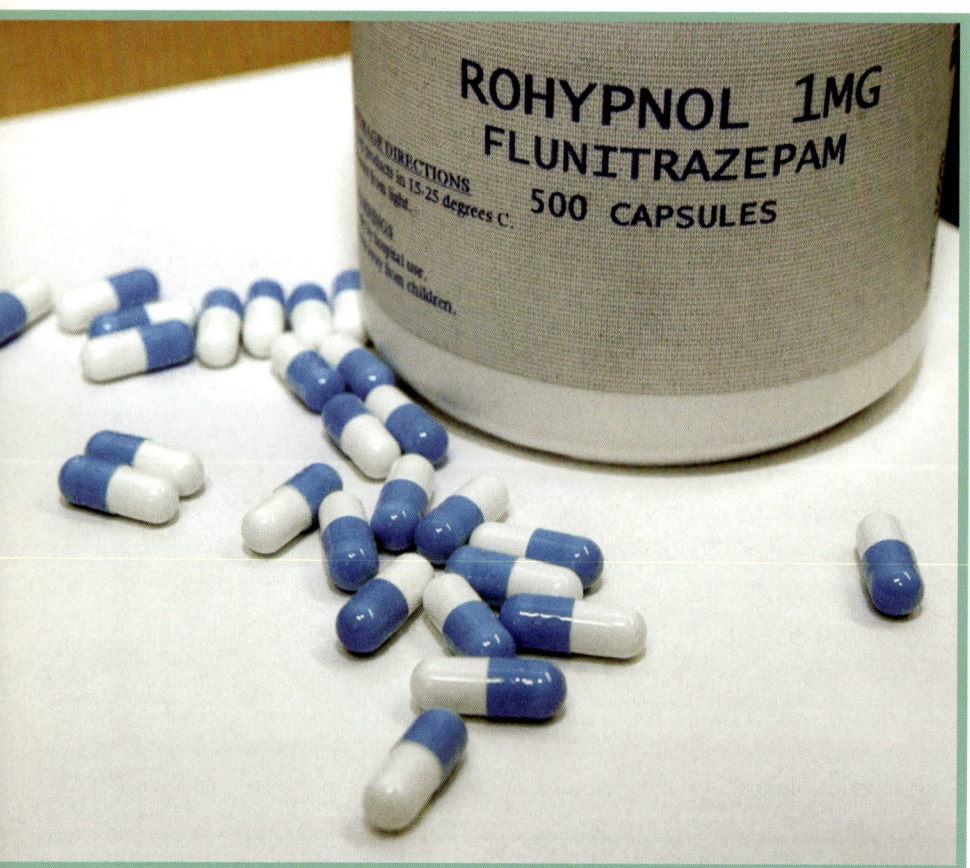

Confiscated Rohypnol pills are photographed in 2003, after Finnish police seized approximately 400,000 pills and materials needed to make one million more pills. Police said the intended market for the drugs was outside of Finland.

is used as a sedative before a **colonoscopy**. In Australia, Rohypnol is used to treat severe insomnia when other drugs have not worked. Yet, because of Rohypnol's negative image as a potential date rape drug, several countries are withdrawing it as a legal medical treatment. Norway, for instance, has withdrawn most Rohypnol

from the market, but it is still available under the brand name Flunipam.

HOW IS ROHYPNOL USED?

Rohypnol is manufactured as white tablets that are distributed in blister packs. Sometimes, counterfeit Rohypnol pills are pinkish or brown. Each pill is scored with either a single line or a cross on one side, and has the word *Roche* or the numbers 1 or 2 on the other side. The number is the number of milligrams of Rohypnol in that particular pill. When it is sold on the street, Rohypnol usually costs less than $5 per tablet. The drug is most often taken orally, but occasionally users grind the pills and either snort the powder or inject it.

When it is dissolved in alcohol, water, or a soft drink, Rohypnol usually has no taste or odor. (Some people do claim that Rohypnol tastes slightly bitter when it is mixed with alcohol.) The user may begin to feel sedated as quickly as 20 minutes after taking the drug. The drug's effects usually peak within two hours but may last as long as eight hours. In some cases, the user experiences impaired motor skills and memory loss as long as 24 hours after taking Rohypnol.

EFFECTS OF ROHYPNOL
Short-term Effects

Rohypnol works by stimulating brain **receptors** that normally bind to the neurotransmitter GABA. When GABA is bound to these receptors, neurons are "turned off" and brain activity goes down.

Rohypnol produces many short-term effects. A user may have drooping eyelids; slow, slurred speech; confusion and dizziness; watery, bloodshot eyes; problems with movement; a lack of inhibition; and memory loss.

A Cosmopolitan cocktail sits on a drink coaster that is used to detect date rape drugs. The coaster has test sensors that turn blue in 30 seconds if a spiked drink splashes on it. Although colleges around the country have bought similar coasters, law enforcement experts warn that the coasters are not always effective and may cause people to have a false sense of security.

Young people often use Rohypnol at raves and clubs because it can produce euphoria or a feeling of drunkenness similar to that produced by alcohol. Others take Rohypnol because they feel it improves appetite and sex drive.

Despite the fact that Rohypnol is a sedative, it can cause users to become excitable or aggressive, even violent, instead of relaxed. But relaxation is much more common, and it is often extreme. A person's breathing and heart rate may drop to dangerously low levels. A Rohypnol user may even have seizures or go into a coma, which can lead to death. These effects are particularly likely when Rohypnol is combined with alcohol, which also slows body functions. Overdose is common when Rohypnol is mixed with alcohol or other sedatives.

Rohypnol as a Date Rape Drug

Because Rohypnol usually causes the user to feel drowsy and confused, it is often used as a date rape drug. Like GHB, Rohypnol can be slipped easily into an unsuspecting victim's beverage by a sexual predator. When the dose is high enough, the victim won't remember what happened after he or she took the drug. The victim also may not remember anything about the sexual predator. In many cases, the only ways the person finds out that he or she has been harmed are if he or she wakes up naked or wakes up in an unfamiliar place. If the person can't remember being attacked, it is difficult for the police to investigate the crime. In addition, Rohypnol remains traceable in the person's urine for around only three days. It often takes at least that long for the victim to understand what has happened and go to the police.

To counter such date rape occurences, in 1998 Hoffmann-La Roche Inc., the company that makes Rohypnol, changed the way the drug is made. Rohypnol pills are now made with a blue dye that will turn any drink blue or cloudy. Rohypnol pills also are more difficult to dissolve. Both of these changes make it harder for people to sneak Rohypnol into drinks.

Long-term Effects

When Rohypnol is used regularly over a long period of time, it can cause both physical and psychological dependence. The person feels the need to use the drug more often to get the same feeling of intoxication that he or she used to get with just a small dose.

TESTING YOUR DRINK FOR DATE RAPE DRUGS

In 2004, a new product was launched in Great Britain. Called the "Drink Detective," it is a matchbox-sized drink testing kit that can detect three of the most common date rape drugs that sexual predators slip into drinks: GHB, ketamine, and Rohypnol. The kit contains test pads for each of the three drugs, as well as pipettes for applying drops of a drink to the pads. For the first time, people going to bars, raves, or clubs could test their drinks for date rape drugs.

According to Bloomsbury Innovations, the manufacturer of the Drink Detective, people will not necessarily have to test every drink. Simply having the Drink Detective with them will likely discourage a sexual predator from attempting to spike the person's drink. The Drink Detective was recognized by *Popular Science* magazine as one of the 100 best new products of 2004.

The central nervous system becomes used to Rohypnol. So when people try to stop taking it, they experience withdrawal symptoms, some of them dangerous. Users may suffer:

- Headaches
- Muscle pain
- Tension
- Confusion
- Irritability
- Severe anxiety
- Numbness and tingling in the arms, legs, fingers, and toes
- Delirium
- Hallucinations
- Convulsions

Even a week after stopping Rohypnol, people can experience seizures or shock. In rare cases, people can die, when the heart and lungs stop working right. Because of the dangers of withdrawal, it is important to seek medical help if you are trying to stop taking Rohypnol.

WHO USES ROHYPNOL?

In general, there are two types of people who use Rohypnol:

- Sexual predators who use the drug to incapacitate their victims
- People who take the drug recreationally

The second group is made up mainly of teens and young adults. They usually combine Rohypnol with alcohol. Many young people who go to raves and clubs also combine Rohypnol with methamphetamine, as a "club drug mix." When it is used as a recreational drug, Rohypnol is almost never taken by itself.

In recent years, Rohypnol use has also become common among teenage gangs. Many gangs require new members to take the drug as part of initiation. Reports also note that teenage girls who hang around with gangs often willingly take Rohypnol. They are then raped by gang members after they pass out.

Occasionally, Rohypnol is used to commit crimes other than date rape. In England, there have been reports of people being robbed after having their drinks spiked with Rohypnol. In addition, some robbers take Rohypnol to make them less nervous while they commit crimes.

Ketamine

On New Year's Eve, Aimee and her boyfriend went to a rave club that they often attended. Hoping for an unusual experience on this holiday, they bought some ketamine and snorted it. They had never tried it before. Before long, the effects kicked in. Aimee remembers having terrifying hallucinations. She saw herself being sucked up by the couch she was sitting on, and she thought the room was turning upside down. Her boyfriend thought Aimee was overdosing. He spent the night sobbing and begging her to forgive him for giving her the ketamine. Aimee doesn't remember most of what happened that night. She does remember that a young woman checked to see whether Aimee had a pulse. When Aimee came to her senses enough to realize where she was, she panicked. She felt as if she had to get out of the club right away. Aimee sprang up from the couch and fell over, but she finally managed to get out of the club. Aimee, who posted her true story online, believes that she would have died—maybe even committed suicide—if she had stayed any longer in the club, feeling the effects of ketamine.

WHAT IS KETAMINE?

Ketamine hydrochloride is a synthetic drug called a **dissociative anesthetic**. It is a very strong hallucinogen. Its physical effects are similar to those produced by PCP (phencyclidine). Ketamine also causes the type of visual hallucinations that are often associated with taking **LSD**.

Ketamine was developed in liquid form in the 1960s as a surgical anesthetic. Physicians often used it for treating soldiers during the Vietnam War. Ketamine is marketed as a **general anesthetic** for both humans and animals, but typically only veterinarians have doses of it.

The powdered form of ketamine was created in the 1970s and was used mainly as a recreational drug. It was not widely used, but it did see some popularity through

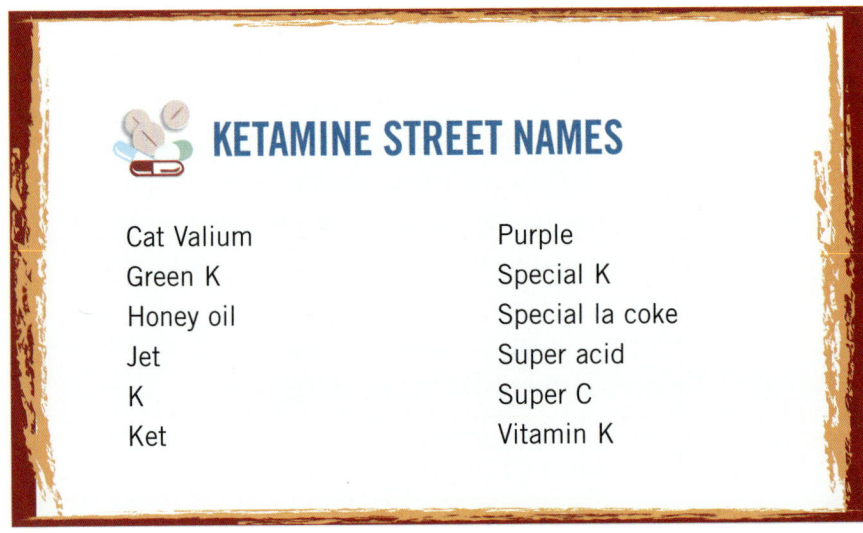

KETAMINE STREET NAMES

Cat Valium	Purple
Green K	Special K
Honey oil	Special la coke
Jet	Super acid
K	Super C
Ket	Vitamin K

Ketamine is a hallucinogenic drug most commonly snorted. The drug was initially developed as an anesthetic for both humans and animals, but now is only legally used for veterinary purposes. Above, one gram of ketamine sits in a single shot nasal dispenser.

the 1980s, when it was nicknamed "Vitamin K." In the 1990s, recreational use of ketamine increased along with the emergence of raves.

Most ketamine used at raves or clubs has been stolen from pharmacies in Mexico. Many young people in the southwestern United States cross the border into Mexico to get ketamine. Over the last several years, many veterinary clinics have been robbed of their supplies of ketamine.

Although ketamine is legally approved for certain medical uses, it is illegal to take it recreationally.

Ketamine is a Schedule III drug, along with drugs such as **anabolic steroids**. Schedule III drugs have legitimate medical uses, but they also can be abused and are addictive.

Legitimate Uses for Ketamine

In addition to its use as a veterinary anesthetic and, in rare cases, as anesthesia for humans, ketamine also has been studied for other legitimate uses. In Russia, researchers have reported that ketamine helps treat alcoholism and phobias.

A 2006 U.S. government study reported that ketamine showed promise as a treatment for depression that works much more quickly than traditional **antidepressant** drugs. The researchers injected 18 depressed patients with liquid ketamine. The patients felt the typical dissociative effects of ketamine, but after those wore off a couple of hours later, the patients reported that their moods had improved dramatically. By the end of the first day of treatment, 71% said they felt significantly better than they had before receiving the ketamine injection. The improvement in mood lasted about a week. It takes about 8 to 10 weeks of treatment with other antidepressants for people to have this type of drastic mood improvement. One of the researchers said that the injected ketamine worked on depressed patients in a way that was almost like "rebooting a computer." According to the study, ketamine works to treat depression by targeting a neurotransmitter called **glutamate**. Most other antidepressant drugs affect serotonin or norepinephrine.

HOW IS KETAMINE USED?

Liquid ketamine is often put into drinks or injected into muscles, never a vein. Injecting the drug is dangerous. If the dose is high enough, the user may become unconscious even before finishing the injection.

The powdered form of ketamine is produced when the liquid form evaporates, leaving behind a white or off-white powder. The powder can be put into drinks, smoked, pressed into tablets, or even sprinkled on tobacco or marijuana and then smoked. When it is made into tablets, ketamine is often taken with other club drugs, including Ecstasy.

People use ketamine as a recreational drug because it can produce a dreamy sensation similar to the high produced by **nitrous oxide**. In higher doses, ketamine has a hallucinogenic effect that can make the user feel separated from his or her body. Some people find the experience uplifting or even spiritual. Sometimes, ketamine makes users lose their sense of time and space and may even make them temporarily forget who they are.

A single dose of ketamine usually costs somewhere between $20 and $25. Such doses called "bumps," are between 10 milligrams and 75 milligrams. Snorting these small lines produces a dreamy effect, often called "K-Land," after about 5 to 10 minutes. A slightly larger dose—60 to 125 milligrams—makes the user feel as if the world is moving in slow motion. The person feels disconnected from his or her surroundings and may have trouble moving. Even larger doses, between 100 and 250 milligrams, produce a near-comatose state that is often referred to as the "K-Hole." Users in this state may lie still and stare into space. Some claim to experience spiritual and life-changing insights. At doses higher than 250 milligrams, the person will be rendered unconscious.

A ketamine high usually lasts one hour, but with larger doses it can last between four and six hours. Even with small doses, it can take as long as 24 to 48 hours for the user to feel normal again.

Some people claim that ketamine makes colors seem brighter and sounds more vivid. Even a small dose of ketamine can increase the heart rate to a dangerous level.

REPORTS OF VETERINARY CLINIC ROBBERIES TO OBTAIN KETAMINE

In July 2001, Dr. Fred Mishrikey, a veterinarian with a practice in suburban Philadelphia, was working at his clinic with his wife, Miriam, who served as his assistant. In the afternoon, two men entered the clinic with a poodle and said that their dog needed treatment. After Dr. Mishrikey examined the poodle, one of the two men pulled out a gun and demanded that the Mishrikeys give him all of the ketamine they had. Miriam showed the two men the cabinet where the ketamine was stored. The men tied up the Mishrikeys with duct tape and fled with the drugs, begging forgiveness as they left.

What happened to the Mishrikeys was not an isolated incident. As ketamine has become more popular as a club drug, a wave of veterinary clinic robberies has spread across the United States. Most of the ketamine sold illegally at clubs and raves comes from veterinary clinics. There have been robberies reported in states all over the country, including Michigan, Colorado, North Carolina, Virginia, Minnesota, and Maryland. In 2000, Illinois police were able to arrest members of a ketamine theft ring that was believed to have robbed several clinics in the Midwest.

Few people have been harmed in veterinary clinic robberies. Many robberies were committed after hours, when

At higher doses, the drug slows a person's breathing and acts as a depressant. This can be extremely dangerous when ketamine is combined with other depressant

Ketamine is a general anesthetic used legally for veterinary purposes but is taken illegally as a recreational drug. Because it's not easy to obtain, there have been many reports of ketamine thefts at veterinary clinics.

the clinics were empty. But veterinarians have become worried about their safety. Many have installed cameras and other surveillance equipment to try to protect themselves and their stocks of drugs.

An officer from Hong Kong's Customs Drug Investigation Bureau holds 50 kilograms of ketamine, seized at Lok Ma Chau, located on the border of China. In the United States, the confiscated drugs would have an estimated retail value of $1.51 million.

drugs, such as alcohol or GHB. Because ketamine is an anesthetic, it prevents users from feeling pain, which can lead people to hurt themselves accidentally while they are high on the drug.

Ketamine also has been known to produce "out-of-body" or "near-death" experiences, even at lower doses than those used by doctors for human anesthesia. A user may feel as if he or she is in a tunnel. Some believe they experience oneness with God or see the future. In some cases, users report that they felt they had died and experienced spiritual things that they could not easily describe.

Some users experience high blood pressure after long periods of use. A few have suffered severe and even fatal breathing problems. Some long-term users have suffered intense stomach pain after heavy usage. Some also have developed urinary tract infections after using very high doses.

Ketamine can be highly addictive. Many users enjoy the changes in consciousness that they experience. They

EFFECTS OF KETAMINE

SHORT-TERM EFFECTS

Ketamine's short-term effects include

- A loss of muscle coordination
- Numbness
- Slurred speech
- Rigid muscles
- Aggressive behavior
- A sense of invincibility or exaggerated strength

LONG-TERM EFFECTS

Common long-term effects of ketamine include

- Amnesia
- Delirium
- Depression
- Memory and thinking problems

begin to use ketamine regularly. Over time, they need larger doses just to achieve a mild, "dreamy" high.

WHO USES KETAMINE?

Ketamine has become extremely popular at dance clubs and raves. The vast majority of ketamine users are teens and young adults. In the 2005 Monitoring the Future Survey, almost 3% of U.S. high school seniors reported that they had used ketamine at least once over the past year. According to the Drug Abuse Warning Network (DAWN), people between the ages of 12 and 25 made up 74% of ketamine-related cases in hospital emergency rooms in the year 2000.

Ketamine is also widely used by sexual predators as a date rape drug. Like Rohypnol and GHB, ketamine can cause a person to lose consciousness. In either its liquid or powdered form, it can be slipped easily into a victim's drink.

6

LSD

Eric had planned his LSD experience weeks before he actually took the drug. Then one night, alone at home, he took four doses of LSD. After 10 to 20 minutes, he felt a powerful rush. Suddenly, everything seemed crisp and clear, and the colors of the objects around him started to swirl around and take on a metallic quality. He felt so happy that he started to laugh. But then, things changed quickly. The room seemed to move and change shape. Although Eric would have brief flashes of clarity, he would rapidly become confused again. At one point, he looked across the room and thought he saw someone standing there, staring at him in horror. It was a hallucination, but it made Eric think he had killed and dismembered someone and been caught by this person who had just come into the house. He felt the sensation of blood dripping from his mouth and became terrified. He tried to call a friend to come help him, but it took him dozens of tries before he could dial the phone correctly. His friend Brian arrived and took Eric to a park. When they got there, Eric became convinced that Brian wanted to take him to the police or the hospital, and Eric began to run. Luckily for Eric, Brian caught up with him and managed to get him home. After a few hours, the LSD wore off, and Eric started to feel a little better. But the experience, which he posted online, had scared him. It scared Brian, too; years later, he still refuses to talk about what happened.

WHAT IS LSD?

LSD, or lysergic acid diethylamide, is the most powerful hallucinogenic substance known to science. It is found in nature, and can be derived from the **ergot** fungus, which grows on rye grass and other grains. However, most of the LSD used as a recreational drug is produced synthetically.

Albert Hoffman, a medical researcher working for the Swiss pharmaceutical company Sandoz, first developed LSD in 1938. Hoffman was looking for new drugs that could be used to stimulate the cardiovascular and respiratory systems. From ergot fungus, he created more than two dozen new substances, including LSD.

Hoffman tested all of the substances, including LSD, but found no medical uses for them. He ignored LSD for five years. In 1943, he accidentally consumed some LSD and experienced psychedelic effects, including dizziness and visual hallucinations. This led him to experiment further with the drug. He prepared a dose of LSD, dissolved it in water, and drank it. Once again, he felt the mind-altering effects of the drug.

Hoffman's work led other scientists to begin experimenting with LSD. Between 1954 and 1962, an American researcher named Oscar Janiger gave the drug to 1,000 volunteers to observe its effects on the mind and body.

Harvard University psychology professor Timothy Leary also experimented with the drug in the 1960s and supported its use.

LSD was studied as a potential treatment for chronic pain and for severe headaches. In addition, the U.S. government experimented with giving people LSD before they took part in military interrogations. But public concern about the dangers of the drug grew. The Senate launched an inquiry into the effects of LSD, and in 1967, the government made the drug illegal.

HOW IS LSD USED?

LSD is sold in liquid form. It may be packaged in small bottles like the ones used for breath-freshening sprays. Usually, though, LSD is sold after it has been applied to absorbent paper, tablets, gelatin squares, or sugar cubes. LSD has no odor or color, but it can have a slightly bitter taste.

LSD and other hallucinogens interfere with the way serotonin, a neurotransmitter, works. Serotonin helps

STREET NAMES FOR LSD

Acid
Back breaker
Battery acid
Blotter acid
Doses
Dots
Elvis
Looney toons

Lucy in the sky
  with diamonds
Mellow yellow
Pane
Superman
Window pane
Zen

TURN ON, TUNE IN, AND DROP OUT

Timothy Leary was a psychology professor at Harvard University during the 1950s and 1960s. At that time, many scientists were studying LSD. Leary began to experiment with the drug, too. He gave it to prison inmates and to some of his students, and he often took it himself. Leary believed that LSD's mind-altering effects could help people achieve spiritual and intellectual awakenings, and he encouraged people to use it. He coined the phrase "Turn on, tune in, and drop out," which became popular among the 1960s counterculture. Leary helped spark the Psychedelic Movement, which was based on using hallucinogenic drugs.

Leary was fired from Harvard in 1963, but he continued to work with LSD even after it was outlawed in 1967. He set up the Castalia Institute in Millbrook, N.Y., where he studied LSD and continued to promote it. He also created a group called the League of Spiritual Discovery (abbreviated LSD, just like the drug) that advocated the use of the hallucinogen.

Leary was sentenced to prison on drug charges in 1971, but escaped and fled to Switzerland. In 1974, the U.S. Drug Enforcement Agency recaptured him. While imprisoned, Leary continued to write about LSD and the counterculture. When he died of prostate cancer at the age of 76 in 1996, he had written more than 27 books and 250 articles. American poet Allen Ginsberg called Leary "a hero of American consciousness."

(opposite page) LSD advocate Timothy Leary holds up a peace sign at a news conference in New York City in 1968. This counterculture icon encouraged LSD use in order to achieve spiritual and intellectual enlightenment.

regulate mood. It also plays roles in regulating behavior, the senses, and muscle control.

Doses of LSD are measured in micrograms—millionths of a gram. The amount of LSD that makes up a typical dose has changed over time. In the 1960s, when the drug was first used recreationally, the average dose was between 200 and 1,000 micrograms. Over the years, doses became smaller. By the 1980s, the typical dose was around 100 micrograms, and by the 1990s, it was between 20 and 80 micrograms. It takes about 25 micrograms of LSD to produce hallucinogenic effects. According to the Drug Enforcement Administration, the standard dose today is around 50 micrograms, although some users take up to 1,200 micrograms.

Users normally start to feel the effects of LSD 30 to 90 minutes after taking the drug. An LSD high—often called a "trip"—lasts about 12 hours, or even longer.

The psychological effects of LSD are especially dramatic. Users experience hallucinations and distortions of reality. People on LSD may become confused or anxious, or they may feel euphoric. They may feel several different emotions at once or have intense and rapid mood swings. Many people report that colors seem more vivid and that their senses seem to "cross over"—that is, users feel as if they can "taste" colors or "see" sounds. For some people, these altered perceptions are terrifying, and they may try to escape from the imaginary dangers they perceive. In a few cases, people have accidentally died while they were high on LSD.

EFFECTS OF LSD

Short-term Effects

It is impossible to predict how LSD will affect a person. The effects depend to a large extent on how much of the drug is taken, as well as the person's mood and surroundings.

LSD produces physical and psychological effects. The physical effects include

- A rise in body temperature
- Dilated pupils
- Increased blood pressure
- Increased heart rate
- Dry mouth
- Sweating
- Tremors
- Chills
- Muscle weakness
- Insomnia
- Nausea
- Goose bumps
- Drooling
- Clenching of the jaw

Long-term Effects

When LSD is used over a long period of time, it may lead users to develop severe mental illnesses, such as depression and **schizophrenia**. The best-known long-term effect of LSD, however, is called a flashback. In a flashback, a person experiences the same hallucinations or altered perceptions that they had during an earlier trip, even if he or she has not taken the drug since that time. Flashbacks can occur weeks, months, and even years after a person has taken LSD. Some scientists believe that people who suffer from other mental illnesses or regularly have used hallucinogenic drugs are more likely to experience flashbacks. But people who have tried LSD only once also have reported flashbacks. Some people experience the same flashbacks over and over again. The psychiatric community considers this phenomenon a psychological disorder. It is called **hallucinogen persisting perception disorder (HPDD)**. Scientists debate whether HPDD is a disorder itself, or just a symptom associated with post-traumatic stress disorder.

LSD is not considered an addictive drug. When people use it regularly, however, they may become psychologically dependent on it. In addition, people may develop a tolerance to the drug and will need to consume larger quantities of it in order to experience the same hallucinogenic effects that they used to achieve with small doses.

WHO USES LSD?

People of all ages use LSD, including older people, many of whom began to use the drug as young adults in the 1960s. LSD is particularly common among teenagers and young adults, who take the drug at raves, dance clubs, or concerts.

According to the 2003 National Household Survey on Drug Abuse, more than 20 million Americans age 12 and older have admitted to using LSD at least once in their lives. The 2005 Monitoring the Future Survey found that 3.5% of twelfth graders had used LSD at some point in the past, while 1.8% had used it within the last year.

CRIMINAL REPERCUSSIONS OF LSD USE

Besides the long-lasting and unpredictable physical and psychological effects of LSD, there is the danger of criminal charges if someone is caught using or possessing LSD. LSD is a Schedule I drug, which means it has a high potential for abuse and has no recognized medical use. Being caught with LSD can result in hefty fines and/or jail time.

Other Club Drugs

Over the past several years, drug use among eighth-, tenth-, and twelfth-grade students has declined by 23%, according to the 2006 Monitoring the Future Survey. However, the survey also found that fewer teens today believe that Ecstasy, LSD, and other drugs are dangerous. In this chapter, we'll look at some of the substances that are emerging as popular club drugs.

2CB

The chemical name for 2CB is 4-Bromo-2, 5-Dimethoxyphenthylamine. This increasingly popular club drug is similar in chemical structure to Ecstasy and mescaline.

In 1974, American chemist Alexander Shulgin first created 2CB. In the 1980s, 2CB became a widely used substitute for Ecstasy at British and American clubs, because it was legal and Ecstasy was not. In July 1995, however, 2CB was placed on Schedule I of the Controlled Substances Act, making it illegal to possess or use. Nonetheless, it remains a relatively common drug at raves and clubs, and is frequently used with Ecstasy to intensify the high.

2CB is sold as a small white pill or as a white powder. Normally, users swallow the drug, but some people snort or smoke powdered 2CB. The typical dose usually ranges from 10 to 40 milligrams.

2CB is a powerful hallucinogen. At lower doses, the high is similar to Ecstasy: euphoria, increased energy, and a feeling of affection and oneness with other people. Larger doses produce a high more like one a person gets from LSD. The person may have intense visual hallucinations that involve color and patterns that seem to appear on ordinary objects or on the faces of other people. Users may also feel an increased sensitivity to touch, tastes, and smells.

2CB usually takes effect about an hour after it is ingested, and the high lasts for three to six hours. If the drug is taken with Ecstasy, the high tends to last a few hours longer. Even after the 2CB has worn off, it takes another two to four hours for the user to start feeling normal again.

There are many physical and psychological effects associated with 2CB. Users may become psychotic, especially if they already have an underlying psychological disorder. Some people also experience panic attacks. Like Ecstasy, 2CB raises the body temperature, often to dangerous levels. Users also may suffer from diarrhea, cramps, and gas, as well as nausea and confusion.

2CB is not considered addictive, but people may develop a tolerance to it if they continue to take the drug regularly over time. Long-term use of the drug can cause severe fatigue, anxiety, and ongoing confusion.

4-MTA

4-MTA, or 4-methylthioamphetamine, is a synthetic stimulant that is chemically similar to **amphetamines** and Ecstasy. Studies claim that 4-MTA is about 6 to 33 times stronger than Ecstasy.

4-MTA was first produced in 1992. Developed by Purdue University chemistry professor David Nichols,

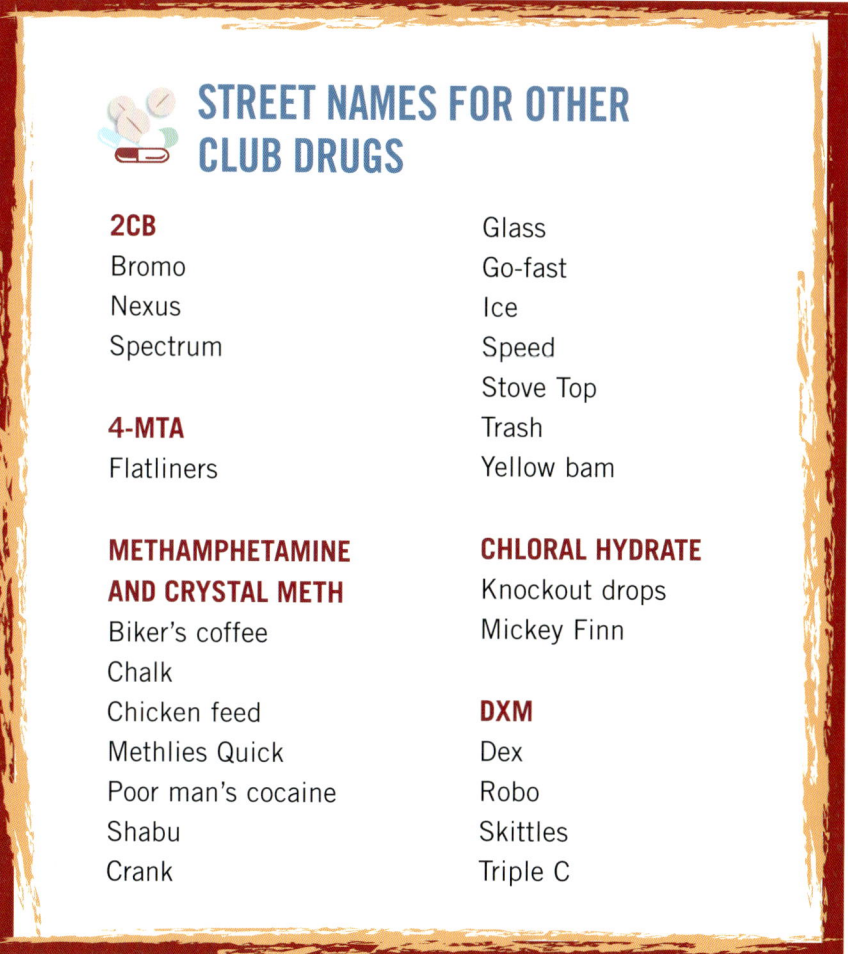

STREET NAMES FOR OTHER CLUB DRUGS

2CB
Bromo
Nexus
Spectrum

4-MTA
Flatliners

METHAMPHETAMINE AND CRYSTAL METH
Biker's coffee
Chalk
Chicken feed
Methlies Quick
Poor man's cocaine
Shabu
Crank

Glass
Go-fast
Ice
Speed
Stove Top
Trash
Yellow bam

CHLORAL HYDRATE
Knockout drops
Mickey Finn

DXM
Dex
Robo
Skittles
Triple C

it was originally intended to be an antidepressant or diet aid. According to Nichols, he and his colleagues had been looking for new drugs that cause the brain to release serotonin, a neurotransmitter related to mood. 4-MTA did, in fact, prove to be a strong serotonin releaser, but it had too many dangerous effects to be considered a useful antidepressant.

During the 1990s, some black-market drug dealers sold 4-MTA to people who wanted to buy Ecstasy. It began to appear in many nightclubs throughout England and the United States, but not everyone who took it liked the high it produced. The drug also was more likely than Ecstasy and other club drugs to cause an overdose. One user described 4-MTA as "not psychedelic, nor really stimulant either. . . . I won't bother again and don't recommend it." Despite negative experiences like this one, people—especially heavy Ecstasy users—continue to use the drug.

4-MTA is usually sold as a cream-colored tablet or pill. It is either swallowed in pill form or ground into a powder and snorted. In rare cases, it is mixed with liquid and injected. The usual dose is around 125 milligrams.

Some of the people who take 4-MTA report that it gives them a high similar to the kind produced by Ecstasy and other amphetamine-related club drugs. Users may experience stimulant effects, including euphoria, an increase in energy, and mild hallucinations. Some also claim that 4-MTA gives them a sense of calmness. The drug's effects can last as long as 12 hours.

There are severe physical risks with using 4-MTA. It is particularly risky to use 4-MTA with other drugs, such as Ecstasy and cocaine. Whether used alone or in combination with other drugs, 4-MTA has been known to cause dangerous cases of hyperthermia that can lead to organ failure and even death. In fact, at least 15 deaths attributed to 4-MTA have been reported in Europe. Despite the dangers associated with the drug, 4-MTA is currently not categorized as part of the Controlled Substances Act in the United States.

METHAMPHETAMINE

Methamphetamine, often called "meth" for short, is a central nervous system stimulant that is extremely addictive. It is available as a powder that can be white, brown, pink, or yellow. In its powdered form, it is usually smoked, snorted, or injected.

Meth can be created using everyday household products, such as over-the-counter cold medicines, ammonia, and battery acid. Meth is on Schedule II of the Controlled Substances Act. This indicates that although the drug can be used medically, it also has a high potential for abuse. Desoxyn, the legal form of meth, is used to treat obesity, narcolepsy, and attention deficit hyperactivity disorder. However, meth is becoming increasingly popular as an illicit club drug. According to the 2005 National Survey on Drug Use and Health, more than 10 million Americans over the age of 12 said they had used meth recreationally.

Meth causes the brain to release large amounts of dopamine, a neurotransmitter which enhances a user's mood and affects movement. People take meth because it produces a feeling of euphoria, often within seconds of taking the drug. Users become energetic and their appetite decreases. Many people feel strong senses of well-being and power, and they are more outgoing and less inhibited. Meth increases heart rate and breathing rate and can cause hyperthermia, paranoia, confusion, convulsions, and sometimes aggression or violence. Some users also experience hallucinations and delusions.

When meth is used regularly over time, it damages the blood vessels in the brain. This damage cannot be reversed. As a result, people who abuse meth often suffer strokes. The brain damage also can cause symptoms similar to those seen with Alzheimer's disease and **epilepsy**. Meth damages brain cells that contain dopamine. Because dopamine plays a role in movement, chronic meth users often develop tics and spasms like those seen in people with Parkinson's disease, a severe movement disorder. Long-time users can have breathing problems and an irregular heartbeat. Malnutrition also occurs because meth makes a user less hungry. Eventually, a user's cardiovascular system may collapse, leading to death.

Crystal Meth

In recent years, a particular form of methamphetamine, called "crystal meth," has become more popular as a club drug. As its name suggests, crystal meth consists of clear, chunky crystals that look like ice or bits of glass. These colorless, odorless crystals are smoked to produce a rapid, long-lasting high. The high is more intense than the high from taking the powdered form of methamphetamine. A crystal meth high may last as long as 12 hours.

Crystal meth users suffer many of the same physical problems as users of powdered meth. However, crystal meth also causes additional physical symptoms, including increased blood pressure and **inflammation** of the lining of the heart. People who take crystal meth often experience psychotic episodes, paranoia, insomnia, and violent behavior. These symptoms may continue for months or even years after the person has stopped taking the drug.

Other Club Drugs

CHLORAL HYDRATE

Chloral hydrate is a synthetic sedative drug that is becoming popular at clubs and raves. First created in 1832, it was the first depressant drug developed to treat insomnia. In the nineteenth century, many alcoholics

METH LABS

Methamphetamine laboratories are by the far the most common type of illegal drug laboratories in the United States today. Two-thirds of all the meth in the United States is created in labs found in Mexico and southern California. The rest of the illegal meth is made in small labs set up in kitchens, garages, vacant buildings, and even the trunks of cars. Meth is relatively easy to produce using common chemicals—including cold and asthma medicines—that can be obtained over the counter.

Because meth labs can operate almost anywhere, they often aren't noticed. This is unfortunate because meth labs frequently explode when the "cooks" who work in them mishandle the hazardous chemicals involved in producing methamphetamine. Most meth labs give off strong chemical smells from the scents of acetone and ammonia. A lab may have a lot of plastic tubing, jars, bottles, and other paraphernalia lying around. The people who live and work in meth labs may seem secretive or unfriendly. Many meth labs receive lots of visitors at odd hours—especially late at night—and most labs produce a great deal of garbage.

took chloral hydrate to help them sleep. However, when chloral hydrate is combined with alcohol, the user loses consciousness quickly. For this reason, chloral hydrate has become a common date rape drug, as well as a recreational drug.

A methamphetamine superlab, capable of producing 90 pounds of methamphetamine, was found and seized in 1995 in Delhi, California. Meth labs are extremely dangerous due to the hazardous chemicals used to make the drug. The increase in methamphetamine labs has unfortunately led to an increase in the number of burn victims.

Chloral hydrate is normally used today as a sleeping pill only if a person cannot take other sleeping pills called benzodiazepines. It is marketed under the brand name Noctec. The drug comes in liquid or capsule form and may be swallowed or inserted into the rectum. Chloral hydrate is listed on Schedule IV of the Controlled Substances Act, which means that it has a legitimate medical use even though it may be abused.

When the drug is taken as recommended by a prescribing physician, it induces sleep but has little effect on blood pressure or breathing. In larger doses, however, chloral hydrate can be dangerous. It can cause nausea and vomiting, stomach pain, dizziness, diarrhea, confusion, anxiety, irritability, and memory loss. In rare cases, it also can produce a serious rash, slow a person's heartbeat, and cause severe breathing problems. If it is used regularly over a long period of time, it may damage the liver. A long-time user of chloral hydrate may have withdrawal symptoms if he or she tries to stop taking it.

DEXTROMETHORPHAN (DXM)

Dextromethorphan (DXM) is a cough-suppressing chemical found in many over-the-counter cough syrups and cold medications. DXM is part of any cold medicine that has the "DM" or "Tuss" in its name. DXM comes in tablets or gel caps. It can also be bought in powdered form, primarily over the Internet.

DXM was first approved for sale as an over-the-counter cough suppressant in 1958. It was considered an improvement over previous cough medicines because it did not make people sleepy. In recent years, it has become increasingly popular as a recreational drug. This is partly because many drug dealers are selling it and passing it off as Ecstasy. DXM is legal, cheaper, and much easier to obtain than Ecstasy. Some pharmacies

Cough syrup containing dextromethorphan (DXM) is on display at a pharmacy in Edmond, Oklahoma. When taken recreationally, DXM is said to produce a buoyant, slightly psychedelic effect. Due to its popularity among club goers and recreational drug users, store owners and retailers have begun moving products containing DXM behind the counter in order to prevent drug theft and abuse.

have moved medications containing DXM behind the counter, making them more difficult to steal.

When taken at the dose recommended for treating a cough (usually between 15 and 30 milligrams), DXM is safe and medically useful. Young adults who abuse DXM as a club drug, however, take doses of around 200 milligrams, which can produce dangerous effects. Some teens have reported drinking three or four bottles of DXM cough syrup in a single day.

DXM acts as a dissociative anesthetic, much like ketamine. The user may feel spaced out and somewhat buoyant, effects similar to those caused by mixing alcohol and opiates or marijuana. DXM also can make the user lose motor control. The person's limbs may begin to feel wobbly, or the person may have trouble moving at all. Higher doses of DXM may produce both visual and audio hallucinations.

There are many dangers associated with the abuse of DXM. Users may feel dizzy and confused, and may experience slurred speech, blurred vision, stomach pain and nausea, or numbness in the fingers and toes. If DXM is used for a long time, it can damage the liver.

DXM becomes even more dangerous when it is combined with other drugs or alcohol. This is frequently done at raves or other parties. When combined with Ecstasy, DXM often results in heatstroke if the user dances for long periods of time. Also, the same liver enzyme processes both DXM and Ecstasy. When the two drugs are taken at the same time, the liver has a hard time breaking down these substances so the body can expel them.

OTHER CLUB DRUGS

In addition to the drugs we have already discussed, other drugs are always being added to the list of those used at raves and clubs. Painkillers, such as OxyContin, and inhalants are among the drugs young people are taking recreationally. Fortunately, the use of many club drugs—including Ecstasy and methamphetamine—has declined in recent years. At the same time, though, a growing number of teenagers are reporting that they don't consider Ecstasy and LSD to be dangerous. For this reason, it remains important to become informed about the dangers of each of them.

Addiction and Treatment

A person is addicted to a substance when he or she continues using it even though it causes problems in daily life. Not all club drugs are physically addictive, but a user can build up a tolerance, which means that he or she needs to take more of a drug to get the same high as when it was first taken.

Kati, a teenage Ecstasy user, explains how she became addicted to the drug. "The first time I tried Ecstasy, I loved it," she says. "I felt like I was part of the in crowd. I felt so happy. . . . Then, one pill didn't work anymore. I had to take as many as 10 pills to get the good feeling. After a while, you're always chasing that first high—but you never get it."

HOW TO TELL IF YOU OR SOMEONE YOU CARE ABOUT HAS A DRUG PROBLEM

It's easy to think you don't have a drug problem if you use Ecstasy or another club drug only when you go to a party. But the more a person takes a drug, the more his or her body begins to feel a need for it. Even if the drug itself isn't addictive, taking it often enough can make the user psychologically dependent on it. Once this happens, everything else in the user's life becomes less important than the need to use the drug.

There are many behavioral warning signs that a person has a problem with drugs. They include

- Dropping grades in school
- A lack of interest in family activities or outings with friends
- Borrowing money more often or in larger quantities than usual
- Mood swings or angry outbursts
- Changes in physical appearance or grooming habits
- Spending a lot of time alone
- Memory problems or a lack of attention

People who are taking drugs also display certain physical and emotional symptoms that may indicate that they have a problem. These include

- A chemical or alcohol smell on the person's breath, body, or clothing
- Confusion, paranoia, or anxiety
- Overreacting to criticism or personal questions
- Being more secretive than usual
- Being hyperactive or more tired than normal

88 ECSTASY AND OTHER CLUB DRUGS

Drug paraphernalia—including pipes, baggies, and a lightbulb—are displayed. Regular drug users may have one or more of the above items and may show emotional signs of drug use such as mood swings, memory loss, and paranoia.

- Gaining or losing a large amount of weight
- Seeming unhappy or depressed
- Talking in a rambling, confused way

In addition to these general warning signs, each type of club drug is associated with specific symptoms. Regular users of hallucinogenic drugs, such as Ecstasy, LSD, and ketamine, may

- Be paranoid or panicked for no apparent reason
- Have trouble distinguishing fantasy from reality
- Exhibit memory loss or problems walking or moving

Depressant club drugs, including Rohypnol and GHB, are linked to:

- Drowsiness and fatigue
- Confusion and disorientation
- Slurred speech
- Depression

Stimulant drugs, such as methamphetamine and crystal meth, may make users:

- Hyperactive
- Lose a lot of weight
- Behave aggressively or impulsively
- Speak too rapidly

If you experience any of these symptoms or notice them in a friend, it may be time to seek help.

TALKING TO SOMEONE ABOUT DRUG ADDICTION

It is often difficult to approach someone if you think he or she has a problem with drugs. In fact, people who are close to drug abusers frequently have trouble admitting that there may be a problem. Drug users tend to believe that they can stop at any time and that there's nothing wrong with what they are doing. It can be easy to believe your friend when he or she tells you everything is okay. But if you are sure the person is abusing drugs, it's important to acknowledge the problem.

The Teen Drug Abuse Web site (http://www.teendrugabuse.us/) has several helpful tips for talking to a friend or family member about addiction. First, you should trust yourself. If you feel certain that something is wrong, you're probably correct. Even if you have some doubts about the situation, it can't hurt to talk to the person. At the very least, you're showing that you care.

Find the right time and place to talk to the person. Bringing up your friend's drug problem in front of a group of people or his or her parents will likely make your friend deny that anything is wrong. In fact, your friend may become angry and refuse to discuss the topic further. Wait until the two of you are alone, in a place

SIGNS AND SYMPTOMS OF SUBSTANCE ABUSE

Teens and young adults who abuse drugs often display different signs, depending on where they are and whom they are with. Here are some of the signs of drug abuse you may notice at home or at school.

At home:

- The person shows a lack of interest in family events.
- The person ignores chores and other responsibilities.
- The person ignores family rules that he or she used to obey.
- Valuable items and money disappear from the home.
- The person doesn't come home on time.
- The person lies about what he or she is doing.
- The person makes many excuses for his or her behavior.

where you both feel comfortable and where you can speak freely.

Be honest about your concerns. Don't be afraid to come right out and say that you think your friend has a problem with drugs. Don't mention rumors you have heard from other people. Stick to talking about what you have noticed and how you feel. Tell the person that you're scared for them or worried about them, but if you are angry or judgmental, the person may get defensive.

- The person uses crude or abusive language.
- Drug paraphernalia (including rolling papers, plastic baggies, or pipes) is found in the person's room or car.
- Prescription drugs are disappearing.
- The person often uses incense or room deodorizing spray (perhaps to mask the smell of smoke).

At school:

- The person's grades drop, or he or she stops turning in homework.
- The person is frequently absent.
- The person falls asleep in class.
- The person defies the authority of teachers and other school staff.
- The person neglects to inform his or her parents about school activities and meetings.

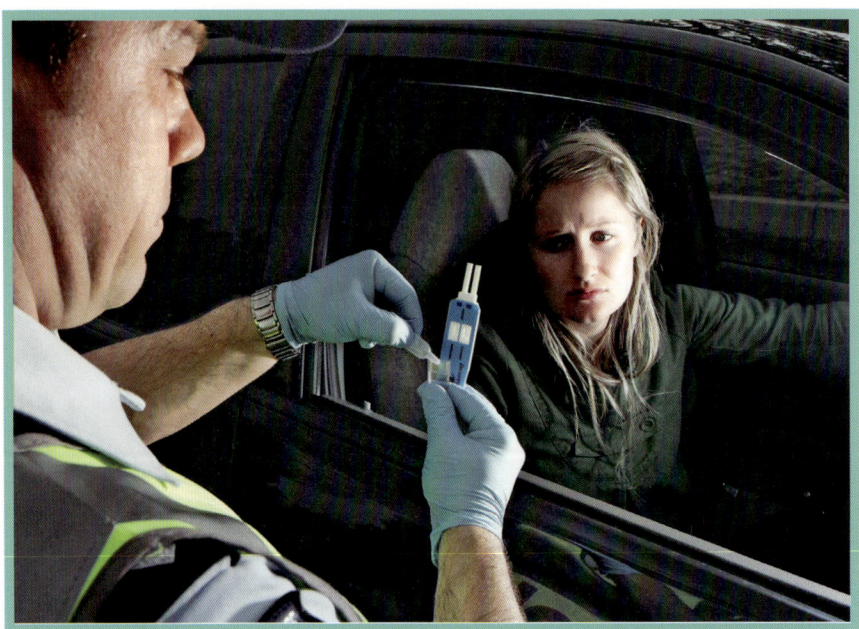

A driver takes a drug test in Melbourne, Australia, as the country becomes the first to begin random roadside drug testing in September 2006. The test can detect Ecstasy, as well as marijuana and speed, in saliva and blood samples.

If the person refuses to admit there is a problem, don't get discouraged. Try again at another time. However, if after several tries you still can't get your friend to speak honestly about his or her drug use, you may need to seek help from a trusted adult, such as a teacher, parent, or counselor. If your friend really does have a serious drug problem, he or she will probably need professional help to deal with the addiction.

TREATMENT FOR DRUG ADDICTION

The goal of treating drug addiction is to help the person stop taking the drug, learn how to function without it, and avoid falling back into the old habit of taking drugs.

WHERE TO FIND HELP

Contact these organizations for help and information.

NARCOTICS ANONYMOUS
P.O. Box 9999
Van Nuys, California 91409
Telephone (818) 773-9999
Fax (818) 700-0700
http://www.na.org/

NATIONAL DRUG ABUSE REFERRAL INFORMATION
(800) 262-2463
www.drughelp.org

NATIONAL INSTITUTE ON DRUG ABUSE
National Institutes of Health (NIH)
6001 Executive Blvd., Room 5213
Bethesda, Maryland 20892-9561
(301) 443-1124
http://teens.drugabuse.gov

PARTNERSHIP FOR A DRUG-FREE AMERICA
405 Lexington Avenue, Suite 1601
New York, NY 10174
212-922-1560
http://www.drugfree.org/

U.S. DEPARTMENT OF HEALTH AND HUMAN SERVICES
Substance Abuse and Mental Health Services
(800) 729-6686
http://ncadi.samhsa.gov/

The National Institute on Drug Abuse estimates that illegal drug abuse costs the United States and its citizens almost $200 billion each year.

Since the 1970s, studies have shown that formal drug treatment programs help drug abusers stop taking drugs, avoid relapsing, and change the destructive behaviors that led them to become addicted to drugs in the first place. According to the National Institute on Drug Abuse, there are several key principles that must be part of a treatment program if it is going to be effective. They include the following:

- No one type of treatment will work for every person.
- Drug treatment needs to be easily available to everyone.
- The treatment should help the person with all aspects of his or her life, not just the drug abuse.
- The treatment program needs to be analyzed and changed as needed over time.
- The person needs to stay in the treatment program for a long enough time to develop new behaviors and ways of thinking.
- Counseling and other behavior-related therapies should be part of any drug treatment program.
- Drug users who also have other mental illnesses should receive treatment that addresses both the addiction and the other psychological disorder in a compatible way.
- Medication to minimize withdrawal symptoms should be used only at the start of addiction treatment. It is not a long-term treatment for drug use.

- Even if the person is forced into treatment against his or her will, the program can be effective.
- The program needs to monitor patients carefully to make sure they are not using drugs while they are undergoing treatment.
- Drug treatment should screen patients for infectious diseases, such as **AIDS** and **hepatitis**. These diseases often are related to drug use.
- Patients may need several episodes of treatment if they are to remain drug free in the long term.

Studies show that drug treatment programs that take these principles into account reduce drug use by 40% to 60%. They also significantly decrease illegal behavior related to drug use, such as stealing.

DIFFERENT TYPES OF TREATMENT
Medication Therapy

The first part of any addiction treatment program is **detoxification**, the process of getting any drugs out of the user's body. This process can be extremely unpleasant for the user. He or she will experience withdrawal symptoms because the body isn't getting a drug that it's used to getting. Among the most common withdrawal symptoms are nausea and vomiting, headaches, irritability, and fatigue. Certain medications can reduce the person's withdrawal symptoms. Sometimes, detoxification can cause withdrawal symptoms severe enough to be fatal if they are left untreated. In such cases, medication is absolutely necessary. For example, GHB causes such dangerous withdrawal symptoms that a person must be under a doctor's care to safely stop taking it.

In some cases, medication also can be used to help restore normal brain function. Methadone often is used to help addicts stop using heroin. Methadone acts on the same areas of the brain as heroin does, so the brain is "tricked" into thinking it has taken heroin even though the user is not actually getting high. As a result, the body's craving for heroin decreases dramatically, which allows the user to function more normally.

Inpatient Treatment

One of the most common programs is inpatient treatment, during which the drug user actually lives at the treatment facility for a set period of time. There is no standard length of time for inpatient treatment. The patient may stay at the facility anywhere from a few weeks to several months.

Perhaps the best-known type of inpatient program is called a "therapeutic community." These residential programs generally keep patients for 6 to 12 months at a time. Everyone at the therapeutic community facility, from the other patients to the staff, is actively involved in the drug treatment program. There are daily activities that help patients examine their behaviors and patterns of thinking, and teach former drug users to reshape their behavior to adapt to a drug-free life.

Outpatient Treatment

Outpatient treatment is where the addicted person receives professional treatment at a facility or clinic but continues to live at home. As with inpatient programs, there is no set period recommended for outpatient treatment. However, according to the National Institute on Drug Abuse, if the patient doesn't participate in a

Residential rehabilitation facilities have become an important part of drug treatment. Director Jack Duffy stands in one of the patients' rooms at Valley Vista, a drug and alcohol treatment center in Bradford, Vermont.

program for at least 90 days, the treatment tends to have little or no effect. Most drug treatment experts recommend that patients who do not take part in an inpatient program continue with outpatient therapy or counseling for months or even years. Many recovering drug addicts remain in outpatient treatment programs for the rest of their lives.

Self-help groups are a well-known aspect of outpatient drug treatment. Organizations such as Alcoholics Anonymous and Narcotics Anonymous are often viewed as extensions of drug therapy and counseling programs.

BEHAVIORAL TREATMENT FOR DRUG ABUSE

Behavioral therapy helps patients cope with their cravings for drugs and learn how to avoid using drugs again. It also helps patients deal with **relapse** if it does occur. Behavior therapy aims to change patients' behavior and to help them learn how to live healthier lives. There are a number of forms of behavioral therapy.

Cognitive Behavioral Therapy

Cognitive behavioral therapy deals not only with behavior but also with the way a person thinks. Its aim is to help patients learn how to recognize why they use drugs in certain situations and to develop ways to avoid falling into drug-using behavior. Cognitive behavioral therapy is based on the notion that the way we learn plays a major role in the development of habits and behaviors. By learning to respond in different ways to situations in which drugs used to play a role, patients can "unlearn" their desire to take drugs and substitute healthier behaviors instead.

The main goal of cognitive behavioral therapy is to prevent relapse. Patients learn to recognize drug cravings and the situations, or "triggers," that make them want to use drugs. They are taught new ways to respond in those situations. By learning how to avoid high-risk situations and cope with cravings, patients learn to live without drugs. According to the National Institute on Drug Abuse, studies show that the strategies learned as part of cognitive behavioral therapy for drug treatment are useful long after treatment has stopped.

Behavioral Therapy for Teens

Behavioral therapy uses a few specific techniques exclusively for adolescents who are trying to overcome drug addiction. Teens are given models for proper behavior, and they receive praise and small rewards as they achieve goals that reflect their new, drug-free behaviors. Often the therapist will give teenage patients "homework" assignments to do, in which they practice the behaviors that will help them avoid using drugs.

One aspect of behavioral therapy for teens is stimulus control. The therapist helps the teen stay away from situations related to drug use, such as clubs and raves, or certain friends. Patients also learn to take part in other behaviors, such as sports and exercise, that aren't compatible with drug abuse. Another aspect of behavioral therapy is urge control. This helps teens recognize the thoughts and feelings that lead them to take drugs. They work to replace those thoughts with positive, healthy thoughts. Yet another aspect of behavioral therapy is social control. This portion of the treatment gets the teen's family members, friends, and other people (such as teachers or coaches) involved in helping the teen avoid using drugs. Often, one of the teen's parents or his or her boyfriend or girlfriend comes to the therapy sessions, too.

Multidimensional Family Therapy for Teens

Like other forms of behavioral therapy, multidimensional family therapy, or MDFT, teaches teenage patients to look at the aspects of their lives that influence their drug abuse. However, MDFT directly involves a teen's entire family in the treatment program. MDFT points out how various people—family members, friends, and the community at large—have an effect on the teen and his or her drug abuse. The therapy allows the whole family to understand why certain situations lead the teen to use drugs. Together, the family learns ways to eliminate drug-using behavior.

As part of MDFT, the teen with the drug problem attends individual therapy sessions, as well as group sessions with his or her family. In the individual meetings, the therapist and teen work on developing better decision-making and problem-solving skills. Teens also learn how to better communicate about how they are feeling. They develop techniques for dealing with stress. The family sessions inform the family about what the teen is learning in individual therapy so that everyone can develop better decision-making skills. In some cases, parents also attend separate therapy sessions, in which they learn to have a positive influence on their teen.

REMAINING DRUG FREE

Stopping drug use and going through the process of detoxification are only the first steps on the long road to a drug-free life. The withdrawal symptoms that go along with quitting drugs can be unpleasant and dangerous. But staying away from drugs in the long term may be even more difficult. People with addictions must learn ways to deal with the situations and feelings that make them crave drugs. Perhaps the most challenging part of drug treatment is recognizing that *any* drug use will likely lead to a relapse. Abstinence is essential.

Recognizing that someone has a drug problem and getting help for that individual are only parts of the anti-drug campaign. Government and social organizations are also working hard to try to stop the spread and abuse of club drugs.

ANTI-CLUB DRUG INITIATIVES

The continuing popularity of club drugs, both as recreational drugs and as date rape drugs, has led many government and community groups to start programs designed to raise awareness about club drugs. In Larimer County, Colorado, a Predatory Awareness Campaign was launched in March 2003. Its goal was to educate local residents about the dangers of date rape drugs, including GHB, Rohypnol, and ketamine. According to Gail Abarbanel of the Rape Treatment Center in Santa Monica, California, an estimated 15% to 20% of sexual assaults involve the use of date rape drugs. The goals of the Predatory Awareness Campaign and many others like it throughout the United States are to make people aware of date rape drugs and how they are used, to teach people how to protect themselves to avoid becoming date rape drug victims, and to educate people about what to do if they suspect they have been the victims of drug-facilitated rapes.

A national program to combat the spread of club drugs was launched by the Drug Enforcement Administration (DEA) in November 2002. Called Operation X-Out, the program aims to inform the American people about the dangers of club drugs and to increase arrests related to Ecstasy and other club drugs. As DEA administrator Asa Hutchinson explained, "The explosive use of Ecstasy and predatory drugs among our youth is fast reaching epidemic levels. Unscrupulous dealers and promoters are marketing Ecstasy, Rohypnol, GHB, ketamine and other lesser known drugs to individuals who, all too often, do not truly understand their potentially devastating effects."

Operation X-Out has several goals:

- To double the number of investigations into club drug cases in the United States
- To increase club drug–related task forces at airports

- To increase DEA resources in the Netherlands, where many club drugs originate
- To create an Internet task force to investigate the sale of club drugs over the Internet

Cooperating with other anti-drug organizations, including Partnership for a Drug-Free America and the Rape, Abuse, and Incest National Network, the DEA hopes to make people more aware of the dangers of club drugs. As Asa Hutchinson put it, "By bringing all shareholders—parents, students, teachers, physicians and treatment professionals—together with law enforcement officials, we will forge solutions at the grass roots level."

Programs like these, along with education about the dangers of drug use, may eventually stop young people from risking their health and even their lives by taking Ecstasy and other club drugs.

GLOSSARY

Acetylcholine   A neurotransmitter that stimulates the brain and helps the skeletal muscles contract.

Addiction   When the body needs a drug or other substance and suffers withdrawal symptoms if it does not get the substance.

AIDS   Acquired immunodeficiency syndrome (AIDS); a condition in which a person's body is unable to fight off illnesses because of a severely weakened immune system.

Alzheimer's disease   A disease that causes the brain to degenerate, causing memory loss and dementia.

Amnesia   A loss of memory caused by injury, shock, disease, or drug use.

Amphetamines   Drugs that act as stimulants on the central nervous system.

Anabolic steroids   A group of synthetic hormones derived from testosterone that are used to promote the growth of muscles.

Anesthetic   A drug that sedates a person or makes a person fall asleep. An anesthetic is used most often for surgical procedures.

Antidepressant   A drug that works to relieve the symptoms of depression.

Benzodiazepine   A drug used to treat anxiety and insomnia.

Bradycardia   A slower than normal heart rate.

Cataplexy   A condition in which the muscles become weak or paralyzed.

Colonoscopy   An examination of the colon using a small camera that is passed through the anus.

CPR   Cardiopulmonary resuscitation; CPR can help start the heart and breathing after a person has suffered cardiac arrest.

Depressant   A drug that slows down the functions of the body.

Detoxification   Freeing the body of drugs.

Glossary

Dissociative anesthetic A sedating drug that causes a person to feel separated from his or her body or from reality.

Dopamine A neurotransmitter in the brain that is related to pleasure and rewards. It is released when people engage in activities such as eating, sex, or drug use.

Empathogenesis A feeling of closeness to other people.

Epilepsy A disorder that causes seizures, convulsions, or brief periods of altered consciousness.

Ergot A black or dark purple fungus that forms on grass or certain grains.

Euphoric Feeling very happy.

Flashback A recurring feeling of hallucinations or altered perceptions experienced during an LSD trip again after a period of time even though he or she has not taken the drug again.

Gamma-aminobutyric acid (GABA) The neurotransmitter in the brain that inhibits behavior.

General anesthetic A drug that causes a person to lose consciousness so that he or she will not feel pain (during surgery, for example).

Glutamate A salt that functions as a stimulating neurotransmitter in the brain.

Hallucinogen A substance that causes hallucinations (perceptions of objects or sounds that are not really there).

Hallucinogen persisting perception disorder (HPPD) A condition in which a person periodically suffers flashbacks from earlier drug experiences.

Hepatitis A disease in which the liver becomes inflamed.

Human growth hormone A natural chemical in the body that makes the muscles grow.

Hyperthermia When body temperature becomes dangerously warm.

Hypothalamus A gland in the brain that controls hunger, thirst, body temperature, and sleep cycles.

Glossary

Inflammation A reaction to injury in which the injured body part becomes red, warm, swollen, and painful.

Insomnia An inability to fall asleep or stay asleep.

Lysergic acid diethylamide (LSD) LSD is a hallucinogenic drug that causes the user to experience sensory distortions and altered perceptions of reality.

Narcolepsy A condition in which a person suddenly falls asleep at random moments.

Neurotransmitter A substance in the brain that sends an impulse, or chemical message, across a nerve cell.

Nitrous oxide Often called "laughing gas"; a sedative often used in dentistry.

Norepinephrine A neurotransmitter that plays a role in focus and attention.

Paranoia A tendency on the part of an individual or group to be excessively or irrationally suspicious or distrustful of others.

Parkinson's disease A disease that causes tremors in resting muscles along with slowed movement, balance problems, and a shuffling walk.

Peripheral vision Seeing something out of the corner, or from the side, of one's eye.

Phencyclidine (PCP) A substance used legally as a veterinary anesthetic and illegally as a psychedelic drug.

Posttraumatic stress disorder A psychological condition that occurs after witnessing or experiencing a traumatic event, such as warfare, a natural disaster, or rape.

Psychedelic Able to produce abnormal mental effects, such as hallucinations or psychotic states.

Psychoactive Affecting the mind or the way a person behaves.

Psychological dependence When someone has developed a habit of taking a drug and becomes mentally distressed when he or she tries to stop taking it.

Glossary

Psychosis A condition in which a person's mind becomes disturbed. A psychotic person will experience hallucinations, delusions, and confused speech and behavior.

Receptors Binding spots on cells. Nerve cells have receptors for neurotransmitters.

Relapse When an addict who has stopped taking drugs starts taking them again.

Schizophrenia A psychological disorder in which a person experiences hallucinations, delusions, and altered perceptions of reality.

Serotonin A neurotransmitter in the brain that plays a role in mood.

Stimulant A substance that speeds up the functioning of the body.

Substantia nigra A part of the midbrain that contains dopamine-producing nerve cells.

Synthetic Produced in a laboratory; not occurring in nature.

Tachycardia A faster than normal heart rate.

Thalamus A part of the brain located at the top of the brainstem that plays a role in motor control and sensory signals.

Tolerance The body's ability to become less responsive to the effects of a drug that is taken over a period of time. When a user has built up tolerance, he or she must take larger amounts of a drug over time to achieve the same effect.

Vertigo A sensation of dizziness in which a person's surroundings seem to spin.

Withdrawal An experience of often painful physical and psychological symptoms that occur when an addict stops taking a drug on which his or her body has become dependent.

BIBLIOGRAPHY

BOOKS

Beck, Jerome, and Marsha Rosenbaum. *Pursuit of Ecstasy: The MDMA Experience*. Albany, NY: State University of New York Press, 1994.

Holland, Julie. *Ecstasy: The Complete Guide: A Comprehensive Look at the Risks and Benefits of MDMA*. South Paris, ME: Park Street Press, 2001.

ARTICLES

"Ecstasy 101: Just the Facts." The National Youth Anti-Drug Media Campaign.

The Expert Advisory Committee on Drugs (EACD). "4-Methylthioamphetamine (4-MTA)." National Drug Policy: A Policy for New Zealand, 1998–2003 (October 2002).

"GHB: A Club Drug to Watch." *Substance Abuse Treatment Advisory* (November 2002).

Leinwand, Donna. "Cities Crack Down on Raves." *USA Today* (2002).

Nolen, R. Scott. "Ketamine Robberies Plague Philadelphia Clinics." *Journal of the American Veterinary Medical Association* (September 15, 2001).

Principles of Drug Addiction Treatment. NIH Publication No. 99–4180 (October 1999).

"Rohypnol: The Date Rape Drug." *BBC News World Edition* (February 4, 1999).

Schonholz, Stephanie. "With Abuse Increasing on Campuses, March Designated for GHB Awareness." *Michigan Daily* (March 20, 2001).

U.S. Food and Drug Administration. "FDA Approves Xyrem for Cataplexy Attacks in Patients with Narcolepsy." *FDA Talk Paper* (July 17, 2002).

Vedantam, Shankar. "Injection May Treat Depression Faster." *The Washington Post* (August 8, 2006).

Bibliography

Wallace-Wells, Benjamin. "The Agony of Ecstasy." *Washington Monthly* (May 2003).

Winstock, A.R., K. Wolff, and J. Ramsey. "4-MTA: A New Synthetic Drug on the Dance Scene." *Drug and Alcohol Dependence* (July 1, 2002).

WEB SITES

"2CB," DrugText Foundation. December 2005. Available online. URL: http://www.drugtext.org/sub/2cb.htm.

"2CB, 2C-i: The Effects, the Risks, the Law," YouthNet UK. Available online. URL: http://www.thesite.org/drinkanddrugs/drugsafety/drugsatoz/2cb2ci.

"4-MTA," Ecstasy.org. November 1998. Available online. URL: http://ecstasy.org/info/4-MTA.html.

"America's Timothy Leary Was FBI Informer," BBC Online Network. June 29, 1999. Available online. URL: http://news.bbc.co.uk/2/hi/americas/380815.stm.

"Beyond Ecstasy: The Facts About Other Club Drugs," National Institute on Drug Abuse. Available online. URL: http://www.drugstory.org/pdfs/beyond_ecstacy.pdf.

Brown University Health Education. "Rohypnol," *Alcohol, Tobacco & Other Drugs*. Available online. URL: http://www.brown.edu/Student_Services/Health_Services/Health_Education/atod/od_rohypnol.htm.

"Chloral Hydrate," Drug Enforcement Administration, U.S. Department of Justice. September 2006. Available online. URL: http://www.dea.gov/concern/chloral_hydrate.html.

"Chloral Hydrate," MedlinePlus Drug Information. U.S. National Library of Medicine and the National Institutes of Health. April 2003. Available online. URL: http://www.nlm.nih.gov/medlineplus/druginfo/medmaster/a682201.html.

"Chloral Hydrate," Victorians' Secret. University of Texas at Arlington. May 2000. Available online. URL: http://drugs.uta.edu/chloral.html.

Bibliography

"Chloral Hydrate (Noctec)," PSYweb.com. Available online. URL: http://psyweb.com/Drughtm/jsp/noctec.jsp.

"Club Drugs," Office of National Drug Control Policy. February 2007. Available online. URL: http://www.whitehousedrugpolicy.gov/drugfact/club/index.html.

"Club Drugs Aren't 'Fun Drugs,'" National Institute on Drug Abuse. June 2005. Available online. URL: http://www.drugabuse.gov/Published_Articles/fundrugs.html.

"Crystal Methamphetamine Fast Facts," National Drug Intelligence Center, U.S. Department of Justice. Available online. URL: http://www.usdoj.gov/ndic/pubs5/5049/index.htm.

D'Angelo, Laura. "'E' Is for Empty: Daniel's Story," National Institute on Drug Abuse. May 2006. Available online. URL: http://teens.drugabuse.gov/stories/story_xtc1.asp.

"The Dangers of Club Drugs," Teen Help LLC. Available online. URL: http://www.teendrugabuse.us/club_drugs.html.

"DEA to Launch Operation X-Out": New Club and Predatory Drug Initiative," Drug Enforcement Administration, U.S. Department of Justice. November 21, 2002. Available online. URL: http://www.dea.gov/pubs/states/newsrel/2002/mia112102.html.

"A Deadly Trip," *Newshour Extra: A Newshour with Jim Lehrer Special for Students*. April 11, 2000. Available online. URL: http://www.pbs.org/newshour/extra/features/jan-june00/ghb.html.

"Dextromethorphan (DXM)," streetdrugs.org, Publishers Group LLC. December 2006. Available online. URL: http://www.streetdrugs.org/dxm.htm.

"Do You Know . . . Rohypnol," Centre for Addiction and Mental Health. December 2006. Available online. URL: http://www.camh.net/About_Addiction_Mental_Health/Drug_and_Addiction_Information/rohypnol_dyk.html.

"Dr. Timothy Leary," Ronin Publishing. Available online. URL: http://www.roninpub.com/TimLea.html.

"Drink Testing Kit for Rape Drug," BBC News. April 6, 2004. Available online. URL: http://news.bbc.co.uk/2/hi/uk_news/3603119.stm.

Bibliography

"Drug Abuse and Addiction: Signs, Symptoms, and Effects." Helpguide.org. Available online. URL: http://www.helpguide.org/mental/drug_substance_abuse_addiction_signs_effects_treatment.htm.

"DXM," The Partnership for a Drug-Free America. Available online. URL: http://www.drugfree.org/Portal/drug_guide/DXM.

"DXM Warning!" DanceSafe. Available online. URL: http://dancesafe.org/documents/druginfo/dxm.php.

"Ecstasy Can Harm the Brains of First-Time Users," Radiological Society of North America. November 2006. Available online. URL: http:// www.rsna.org/rsna/media/pr2006-2/ecstasy-2.cfm.

"Ecstasy (MDMA) and Club Drugs," Focus Adolescent Services. Available online. URL: http://www.focusas.com/Ecstasy.html.

Erowid Experience Vaults. Accessed November 27, 2006. Available online. URL: http://www.erowid.org.

"Gamma Hydroxybutyrate (GHB)," Executive Office of the President, Office of Drug Control Policy. *ONDCP: Drug Policy Information Clearinghouse Fact Sheet*. November 2002. Available online. URL: http://www.streetdrugs.org/pdf/GHBondcp.pdf.

"Gamma Hydroxybutyrate (GHB)," Ellen Kuwana. Neuroscience for Kids. June 2005. Available online. URL: http://faculty.washington.edu/chudler/ghb.html.

"GHB Approved to Treat Symptom of Narcolepsy," Ellen Kuwana. Neuroscience for Kids. July 2002. Available online. URL: http://faculty.washington.edu/chudler/ghbn.html.

"Ketamine," Drug Enforcement Administration, U.S. Department of Justice. September 2006. Available online. URL: http://www.dea.gov/concern/ketamine_factsheet.html.

"Ketamine," National Youth Anti-Drug Media Campaign. Available online. URL: http://www.theantidrug.com/drug_info/drug_info_ketamine.asp.

Bibliography

"Ketamine," www.streetdrugs.org, Publishers Group LLC. December 2006. Available online. URL: http://www.streetdrugs.org/ketamine.htm.

"Ketamine Dosage," *The Good Drugs Guide.* January 2006. Available online. URL: http://www.thegooddrugsguide.com/ketamine/dosage.htm. Accessed November 29, 2006.

"Ketamine Fast Facts," National Drug Intelligence Center, U.S. Department of Justice. Available online. URL: http://www.usdoj.gov/ndic/pubs4/4769/index.htm.

Kuwana, Ellen. "Rohypnol," Neuroscience for Kids. May 2005. Available online. URL: http://faculty.washington.edu/chudler/roof.html.

"LSD," Drug Enforcement Administration, U.S. Department of Justice. August 2006. Available online. URL: http://www.dea.gov/concern/lsd.html.

"LSD," National Youth Anti-Drug Media Campaign. Available online. URL: www.theantidrug.com/drug_info/drug_info_lsd.asp.

"LSD," Neuroscience for Kids. August 2005. Available online. URL: http://faculty.washington.edu/chudler/lsd.html.

"LSD," streetdrugs.org, Publishers Group LLC. December 2006. Available online. URL: http://www.streetdrugs.org/lsd.htm.

"LSD Fast Facts," National Drug Intelligence Center, U.S. Department of Justice. Available online. URL: http://www.usdoj.gov/ndic/pubs4/4260/index.htm.

"MDMA/Ecstasy Research: Advances, Challenges, Future Directions," National Institute on Drug Abuse. July 2001. Available online. URL: http://www.drugabuse.gov/Meetings/MDMA/MDMAExSummary.html.

"Methamphetamine," National Youth Anti-Drug Media Campaign. Available online. URL: http://www.theantidrug.com/drug_info/drug_info_meth.asp.

"Methamphetamine," Office of National Drug Control Policy. March 2007. Available online. URL: http://www.whitehousedrugpolicy.gov/drugfact/methamphetamine.

Bibliography

"Monitoring the Future Survey, Overview of Findings 2006," National Institute on Drug Abuse. February 2007. Available online. URL: http://www.drugabuse.gov/newsroom/06/MTF06Overview.html.

Narcotic Educational Foundation of America. "Rohypnol: The Date Rape Drug," Available online. URL: http://www.cnoa.org/N-12.pdf.

"NIDA InfoFacts: LSD," National Institute on Drug Abuse. May 2006. Available online. URL: http://www.drugabuse.gov/infofacts/lsd.html.

"NIDA InfoFacts: Methamphetamine," National Institute on Drug Abuse. March 2007. Available online. URL: http://www.nida.nih.gov/Infofacts/methamphetamine.html.

"NIDA InfoFacts: Treatment Approaches for Drug Addiction," National Institute on Drug Abuse. August 2006. Available online. URL: http://www.nida.nih.gov/infofacts/treatmeth.html.

"Other Club Drugs," *eMedicineHealth*. October 2005. Available online. URL: http://www.emedicinehealth.com/club_drugs/page8_em.htm.

Partnership for a Drug-Free America. *Meth360 Information Kit*. Available online. URL: http://www.drugfree.org/Files/Meth_Fact_Sheets.

"Predatory Drug Awareness Campaign," Drug Enforcement Administration, U.S. Department of Justice. March 3, 2003. Available online. URL: http://www.dea.gov/pubs/states/newsrel/2003/denver030303.html.

"Psychedelic '60s: Timothy Leary," University of Virginia. Available online. URL: http://www.lib.virginia.edu/small/exhibits/sixties/leary.html.

"Rave: A Profile of the Ecstasy User." Available online. URL: http://www.siena.edu/boswell/Drug%20Projects/MDMA/RAVE.htm. Accessed November 29, 2006.

"Raves," Drug Enforcement Administration, U.S. Department of Justice. September 2006. Available online. URL: http://www.dea.gov/ongoing/raves.html.

Bibliography

"Rohypnol, the Date Rape Drug," MedicineNet.com. November 2002. Available online. URL: http://www.medicinenet.com/script/main/art.asp?articlekey=21794.

"Statistics on Teenage Drug Use," Teen Help LLC. Available online. URL: http://www.teendrugabuse.us/teen_drug_use.html.

"Street Terms: Drugs and the Drug Trade," Office of National Drug Control Policy. August 2006. Available online. URL: http://www.whitehousedrugpolicy.gov/streetterms/.

"Talking to Teens About Addiction," Teen Help LLC. Available online. URL: http://www.teendrugabuse.us/teen_addiction.html.

"Teens and the Drug Ecstasy," Teen Help LLC. Available online. URL: http://www.teendrugabuse.us/ecstacy.html.

"Trials of Ecstasy for Post Traumatic Stress to Include U.S. Soldiers," Common Sense for Drug Policy. Available online. URL: http://www.csdp.org/news/news/ecstasynews.htm.

"What Is Ketamine?" DanceSafe. Available online. URL: http://www.dancesafe.org/documents/druginfo/ketamine.php.

"What Parents Should Know About Ecstasy," KidsGrowth.com. Available online. URL: http://kidsgrowth.com/resources/articledetail.cfm?id=880.

Witmer, Denise. "Warning Signs of Teenage Drug Abuse," About.com: Parenting of Adolescents. Available online. URL: http://parentingteens.about.com/cs/drugsofabuse/a/drug_abuse20.htm.

"Worldwide Raver's Manifesto Project, Toronto," Ecstasy.org. Available online. URL: http://ecstasy.org/experiences/trip98.html.

FURTHER READING

Adams, Colleen. *Rohypnol: Roofies—The Date Rape Drug*. New York: Rosen, 2006.

Balkin, Karen F. *Club Drugs*. San Diego, Calif.: Greenhaven Press, 2004.

Kehner, George B. *Date Rape Drugs*. Philadelphia: Chelsea House Publishers, 2004.

Lockwood, Brad. *Ketamine: Dangerous Hallucinogen*. New York: Rosen, 2006.

Marcovitz, Hal. *Club Drugs*. San Diego, Calif.: Lucent Books, 2006.

———. *Methamphetamines*. San Diego, Calif.: Lucent Books, 2005.

Swarts, Katherine, ed. *The History of Drugs: Club Drugs*. San Diego, Calif.: Greenhaven Press, 2005.

Wolf, Marie. *GHB and Analogs: High Risk Club Drugs*. New York: Rosen, 2006.

WEB SITES

CLUBDRUGS.ORG: IMPORTANT INFORMATION AND RESOURCES ON CLUB DRUGS

The National Institute on Drug Abuse (NIDA) sponsors this site. It offers comprehensive articles on the dangers of club drug abuse, as well as current statistics and trends regarding its use. The site also provides additional links to drug-related information.

http://www.clubdrugs.org/

DRUG ENFORCEMENT ADMINISTRATION: *OPERATION X-OUT*, ECSTASY AND PREDATORY DRUGS

This site, maintained by the U.S. Drug Enforcement Administration (DEA), instructs viewers on the devastating effects of Ecstasy and predatory (date rape) drugs. Learn of DEA campaigns to stop drug abuse and find in-depth descriptions of various club drugs.

http://www.dea.gov/concern/clubdrugs.html

DRUG ENFORCEMENT ADMINISTRATION (DEA): DEA DEMAND REDUCTION: STREET SMART PREVENTION

Get the latest drug information at this "street-smart" site, targeted to teens. Read about the negative effects of drug abuse on the individual, his or her personal relationships, and the environment. The reader can also browse links on illegal and prescription drugs.

http://www.justthinktwice.com

NATIONAL INSTITUTE ON DRUG ABUSE: NIDA INFOFACTS: CLUB DRUGS

Browse the official Web site of the National Institute on Drug Abuse and its collection of information related to club drugs. Readers can find up-to-date medical and health-related information on the use of club drugs. The site also suggests additional publications and resources for parents, teachers, and students.

http://www.nida.nih.gov/Infofacts/clubdrugs.html

NATIONAL YOUTH ANTI-DRUG MEDIA CAMPAIGN: CLUB DRUGS

This is a comprehensive site that describes types of club drugs and offers advice for parents if they think their teens are using such drugs. There are additional links to specific kinds of drugs, current research, and consequences of abuse.

http://www.theantidrug.com/drug_info/drug_info_clubdrugs.asp

OFFICE OF NATIONAL DRUG CONTROL POLICY: FACTS & FIGURES: CLUB DRUGS

Learn of the national drug control policy as implemented by the White House of the United States. Find information on the 1988 Anti–Drug Abuse Act and other pertinent government initiatives to cap illegal drug use.

http://www.whitehousedrugpolicy.gov/drugfact/club/index.html

PHOTO CREDITS

PAGE

13: AP Images
18: U.S. Drug Enforcement Administration
22: © Jeff Minton/Corbis
24: U.S. Drug Enforcement Administration
28: © Scott Houston/Corbis
37: AP Images
43: © Floris Leeuwenberg/The Cover Story/Corbis
44: AP Images
50: AFP/Getty Images
52: AP Images
59: © David Hoffman Photo Library/Almay
63: © PYMCA/Almay
64: AFP/Getty Images
70: AP Images
82: AP Images
84: AP Images
88: Getty Images
92: Getty Images
97: AP Images

COVER
Courtesy of the U.S. Drug Enforcement Administration

INDEX

A

abstinence from drugs, 100
abuse. *See* drug abuse
addiction
    drug abuse and, 18–19
    ketamine and, 65–66
    talking to someone about, 89–92
    See also treatment for addiction
AIDS, 95
alcohol, 48
    combined with drugs, 38, 55, 85
    drink testing kit, 54
    overdoses and, 53
"alcohol-free" party description, 14
Alcoholics Anonymous, 97
Alzheimer's disease, 30, 80
amphetamines, 77, 78
anabolic steroids, 60
anesthetic, 16, 58, 60, 64, 84
antidepressant drug, 60, 78
anti-drug campaign, 100–102

B

behavioral therapy, 98–100
behavioral warnings, drug abuse, 87
benzodiazepine, 16, 83
black market drug dealers, 78
Bloomsbury Innovations, 54
brain
    damage, by Ecstasy, 29, 30
    parts of, 36
    See also neurotransmitter systems
"bumps," 61
"burnout" effect, 25

C

cartoon characters on drugs, 23–24
Castalia Institute, 71
cataplexy, 38
central nervous system depressant, 15, 36, 46
central nervous system stimulant, 21, 79, 89
chloral hydrate, 18, 77, 81–83
Clinton, President William, 45
club drugs, 15–18
    decline in use of, 85
    emerging, 75
    introduction to, 12–19
    places used, 14
    street names for, 77
    See also drug mixing
cocaine, 31, 48, 78
cognitive behavioral therapy, 98
Controlled Substances Act, 32–33, 76, 79, 83
Convention of Psychotropic Substances (1971), 48
cough suppressant. *See* DXM
counterculture of 1960s, 71
crack cocaine, 31, 48
"crashing," 25
crimes, drug usage and, 56, 74, 95
criminal prosecution, 31
crystal meth, 77, 80, 89

D

dance club. *See* rave
date rape drug
    anti-club drug campaign and, 100–101
    chloral hydrate as, 82
    drink testing kit, 54
    GHB as, 15–16, 42–46
    ketamine as, 16–17, 66
    Rohypnol as, 48, 50, 53–54
    See also sexual assault
Date-Rape Drug Prohibition Act of 2000, 45
de Win, Maartje, 29
DEA. *See* U.S. Drug Enforcement Agency
Depressant. *See* central nervous system depressant
depressant drugs, 63, 81, 89
Desoxyn, 79
detoxification program, 40, 95–96
dextromethorphan. *See* DXM
dietary supplement, 36
dissociative anesthetic, 58, 84
dopamine activity, 25, 39, 79, 80
"Drink Detective," 54
drink spiking. *See* date rape drug
drug abuse
    addiction and, 18–19
    signs and symptoms, 90–91
    See also Controlled Substances Act
Drug Abuse Warning Network (DAWN), 66
drug addiction. *See* addiction
drug cravings, 98
drug dealers, 34, 78
Drug Enforcement Administration (DEA), 42, 71, 72, 101, 102
drug mixing, 40, 42
    4-MTA and, 78
    alcohol and, 38, 55, 85
    "club drug mix," 55–56, 61
drug paraphernalia, 91
drug problem warning signs, 87–89
drug treatment centers, 30, 31
Drug-Induced Rape Prevention and Punishment Act (1996), 49
DXM (dextromethorphan), 17, 77, 83–85

E

Ecstasy, 20–34
    2CB compared to, 75
    4-MTA compared to, 77, 78
    abuse, dependence and, 30–31
    common effects of, 25
    dangers of usage, 31, 34
    decline in use of, 85
    described, 15, 21–23
    dosages, 23
    DXM passed off as, 83
    ketamine and, 61
    long-term physical effects, 28–30, 88
    raves and, 13
    in scientific experiments, 23
    short-term physical effects, 25–28
    street names for, 26, 27
    symbols stamped on, 23–24
    U.S. banning of, 22
    usage methods, 23–25
    user profiles, 29, 31
emotional symptoms, drug abuse, 87–88
empathogenesis, 25
epilepsy, 80
ergot fungus, 68
euphoria, 12, 53, 72, 79

Index

F
flashbacks
   LSD and, 17, 73
   posttraumatic stress disorder and, 23
Flunipam, 51
Food and Drug Administration (FDA), 37–38
4-Bromo-2, 5-Dimethoxyphenthylamine, 75
4-MTA, 18, 77–79

G
gamma hydroxybutyrate. *See* GHB
gamma-amniobutyric acid (GABA), 36, 51
gangs, 56
general anesthetic, 58
GHB (gamma hydroxybutyrate), 15–16, 35–46
   alcohol and, 38, 40
   as date rape drug, 42–46
   dosages, 38
   long-term physical effects, 40, 89
   short-term physical effects, 39–40
   street names for, 39
   usage methods, 38
   user profile, typical, 41–42
   withdrawal symptoms, 40
GHB Awareness Month, 41
Ginsberg, Allen, 71

H
hallucinogen persisting perception disorder (HPDD), 73–74
hallucinogenic effects, 21, 38, 57, 61, 76, 85, 88. *See also* LSD
Harvard University, 69, 70
hepatitis, 95
heroin, 31, 48, 96
hiding of drugs, 15
Hillory J. Farias and Samantha Reid Date-Rape Drug Prohibition Act of 2000, 45
"hippies," 17, 70–71
Hoffman, Albert, 68
Hoffman-La Roche Inc., 48, 53
human growth hormone, 36
Hutchinson, Asa, 101, 102
hyperthermia, 27

I
illegal drugs. *See* club drugs
impure pills, 34
inhalants, 85
insomnia, 16, 29, 50
Internet. *See* Web site

J
Janiger, Oscar, 68

K
ketamine (ketamine hydrocloride), 16–17, 57–66, 84
   described, 58–60
   effects of, 65, 88
   legitimate uses for, 60
   as Schedule III drug, 60
   street names for, 58
   usage methods, 60–66
   user profile, typical, 66
"K-Hole," 61
"K-Land," 61

L
League of Spiritual Discovery, 71
Leary, Timothy, 69, 70–71
LSD (lysergic acid diethylamide), 17, 58, 67–74, 85
   described, 68–69
   dosages, 72
   long-term physical effects, 73–74, 88
   short-term physical effects, 72–73
   street names for, 69
   usage methods, 69, 72
   user profile, typical, 74

M
marijuana, 48, 85
MDMA. *See* Ecstasy
Merck, 21
mescaline, 75
meth labs, 81–82
methadone, 96
methamphetamine ("meth"), 15, 17, 55, 79–80
   crystal meth, 77, 80
   decline in use of, 85
   effects of, 89
   street names for, 77
methylenedioxymethamphetamine. *See* Ecstasy
Mexico, 47, 49, 59
military interrogations, 69
Monitoring the Future Survey, 41–42, 66, 74, 75
mood, 25, 60, 78. *See also* serotonin levels
multidimensional family therapy, 99–100
Multidisciplinary Association for Psychedelic Studies (MAPS), 23

N
names for drugs. *See* street names
narcolepsy, 38, 42, 79
Narcotics Anonymous, 93, 97
National Drug Abuse Referral Information, 93
National Drug Intelligence Center (NDIC), 46
National Household Survey on Drug Abuse, 74
National Institute on Drug Abuse, 31, 93, 94, 96–97, 98
National Survey on Drug Use and Health, 79
"near-death" experience, 64
neurotransmitter systems, 25, 39, 51, 60, 69, 78, 79
Newshour PBS program, 42
Nichols, David, 77, 78
nitrous oxide, 61
Noctec, 83
norepinephrine, 25

O
Operation X-Out, 101–2
opiates, 85
organizations, addiction treatment, 92–95
"out-of-body" experience, 64
overdoses, 57
   alcohol and, 53
   impure pills and, 34
OxyContin, 85

Index

P
painkillers, 85
Parkinson's disease, 21
Partnership for a Drug-Free America, 93, 102
party. *See* rave
PCP (phencyclidine), 17, 58
phencyclidine. *See* PCP
physical symptoms, drug abuse, 87–88
posttraumatic stress disorder (PTSD), 23
Predatory Awareness Campaign, 101
predatory drugs. *See* date rape drugs
psychedelic drug, 18
Psychedelic Movement, 71
psychiatric therapy, MDMA and, 22
psychological dependence on drug, 19, 30, 74, 87
psychological disorder, 73, 76
psychosis, 17
Purdue University, 77

R
Radiological Society of North America (RSNA), 29
rape, 56. *See also* date rape drug; sexual assault
Rape, Abuse, and Incest National Network, 102
rave
    atmosphere of, 12
    cracking down on, 14
    ketamine usage at, 66
    origin of, 13
    Rohypnol usage at, 53
RAVE (Reducing Americans' Vulnerability to Ecstasy) Act, 14
Reid, Samantha, 42–45
relapse, 98
robbery, drug related, 31, 62, 95
Rohypnol (flunitrazepam), 16, 47–56, 48
    as date rape drug, 48, 53–54
    described, 48–51
    dosages, 51
    long-term physical effects, 54–55, 89
    short-term physical effects, 51–53
    street names for, 49
    user profile, typical, 55–56
    withdrawal symptoms, 55

S
Sandoz, 68
Schedule I drug
    2CB as, 76
    described, 32
    Ecstasy as, 31
    GHB as, 37, 45
    LSD as, 74
    Rohypnol considered for, 49
Schedule II drug, 32, 79
Schedule III drug, 32–33, 48, 60
Schedule IV drug, 33, 48, 83
Schedule V drug, 33
schizophrenia, 73
scooping, 44
sedative, 50, 53
self-help groups, 97
serotonin levels, 25, 39, 60, 69, 72, 78
sexual assault, 46. *See also* date rape drug
sexual predator, 48, 53
    drink testing kit and, 54
    ketamine and, 16, 66
Predatory Awareness Campaign, 101
Rohypnol and, 55
See also date rape drug
Shulgin, Alexander, 22, 75
signs and symptoms, drug abuse, 90–91
sleeping pill, 49, 83
stealing drugs, 62
stealing for drug payment, 31, 95
stimulant. *See* central nervous system stimulant
street names
    club drugs, 77
    for Ecstasy, 26, 27
    for GHB, 39
    for ketamine, 58
    for LSD, 69
    for Rohypnol, 49
substance abuse. *See* drug abuse; specific substance

T
Teen Drug Abuse Web site, 89
teen therapy, drug abuse, 98–100
    behavior therapy, 98–99
    multidimensional family therapy, 99–100
"therapeutic community," 96
therapy for drug abuse, 98–100
tolerance for drug, 19
treatment for addiction, 92–100
    behavioral treatment, 98–100
    cognitive behavior therapy, 98
    drug-free living, 100
    hotlines, 93
    inpatient treatment, 96
    key program principles, 94–95
    medication therapy, 95–96
    outpatient treatment, 96–97
    self-help groups, 97
    teen behavior therapy, 98–99
treatment for drug abuse, 86–102
"triggers" for drug abuse, 98
"trip" (high), 72
"truth serum," 21
2CB, 18, 75–77

U
University of Michigan Monitoring the Future Survey, 41–42
U.S. Department of Health and Human Services, 93
U.S. Drug Enforcement Administration (DEA), 42, 71, 72, 101, 102
U.S. government, 69

V
Valium, 48
veterinarians, 16, 58, 59, 60, 62–63
Vietnam War, 58
"Vitamin K," 59

W
Web site, 31, 40, 42, 89, 93
withdrawal symptoms, 19, 40, 55, 95–96
World War I, 21

X
Xylem, 42
Xyrem, 38

ABOUT THE AUTHORS

TARA KOELLHOFFER earned her dual bachelor's degrees in political science and history from Rutgers University. Today, she is a freelance writer and editor with more than 10 years of experience working on nonfiction books, covering topics ranging from social studies and biography to health and science. She has edited hundreds of books and teaching materials, including a history of Italy published by Greenhaven Press and the *Science News for Kids* series published by Chelsea House. She lives in Pennsylvania with her husband Gary.

Series introduction author **RONALD J. BROGAN** is the Bureau Chief for the New York City office of D.A.R.E. (Drug Abuse Resistance Education) America, where he trains and coordinates more than 100 New York City police officers in program-related activities. He also serves as a D.A.R.E. regional director for Oregon, Connecticut, Massachusetts, Maine, New Hampshire, New York, Rhode Island, and Vermont. In 1997, Brogan retired from the U.S. Drug Enforcement Administration (DEA), where he served as a special agent for 26 years. He holds bachelor's and master's degrees in criminal justice from the City University of New York.